THE CALICO CAT AT
the Chibineko
Kitchen

First published in Great Britain in 2025 by John Murray (Publishers)

Original Japanese edition published in 2020 by Kobunsha Co. Ltd., Tokyo
Chibinekotei No Omoidegohan: Mikeneko to Kinou no Curry

SRD

English language translation rights arranged through
The English Agency (Japan) Ltd. and New River Literary Ltd.

Extract from the Koitozairai Farmers' Club website reprinted with permission
from the Koitozairai Farmers' Club, Kimitsu Agricultural Cooperative.

A CIP catalogue record for this title is available from the British Library

Paperback ISBN 9781399817660
ebook ISBN 9781399817691

Typeset in Baskerville MT by Hewer Text UK Ltd, Edinburgh

Printed and bound in India by Manipal Technologies Limited, Manipal

John Murray policy is to use papers that are natural, renewable and
recyclable products and made from wood grown in sustainable forests.
The logging and manufacturing processes are expected to conform
to the environmental regulations of the country of origin.

Carmelite House
50 Victoria Embankment
London EC4Y 0DZ

www.johnmurraypress.co.uk

John Murray Press, part of Hodder & Stoughton Limited
An Hachette UK company

THE CALICO CAT AT
the Chibineko
Kitchen

YUTA TAKAHASHI

Translated by
CAT ANDERSON

JOHN MURRAY

1

A black cat and miso-marinated tofu

小糸在来®
Koitozairai soybeans

These soybeans are lovingly cultivated in the catchment basin of the Koitogawa River in Kimitsu, Chiba Prefecture. They are of the highest quality, on a par with black tanbaguro soybeans, and have a subtle aroma and a simple, sweet taste with no bitterness. Soybeans with the Koitozairai trademark are valued by buyers as holding their own against Hokuriku and Tohoku chamame beans when it comes to flavour.

Koitozairai Farmers' Club,
Kimitsu Agricultural Cooperative

My name is Nagi Hayakawa.

'Nagi' means 'the calm out at sea'. My mother loved the sea so much she named me after it. Though her illness made her so frail she couldn't even swim, she always used to say that she found the sound of the waves soothing.

So much so, that she chose to spend her final days by the seashore, in a large hospital in Chiba Prefecture. Fifteen years ago, in a room with a view of the water, she drew her last breath listening to the waves.

I was five years old.

I'll probably end up in the same hospital sooner or later, with the sound of the same waves in my ears. Like my mother, I have a serious illness. I've been told it's terminal, and that, at twenty years old, I have five years left to live.

'Just my luck . . .' I muttered when I was given the news. I was deliberately keeping my words light, but it didn't help: nothing was going to make me feel better. All sorts of thoughts crossed my mind in that moment: *Is there any point in going into hospital? Is there even any point in continuing to live, when I know it's all going to end so soon? Was there any point in being born at all? When was it all decided? Could I have lived a different life, one in which I never got ill – or was my fate set in stone the moment I came into this world?*

2

No matter how long I turned it over in my mind, I just couldn't make sense of it. And all the while, the time I had left was slipping away.

One December morning, Nagi made her way to that seaside town. She was heading not to the hospital, but to a restaurant by the water.

Outside the station, she climbed into a taxi, following directions she had memorised. The cab drove along the quiet riverside road that led towards the sea, until Tokyo Bay came into view.

'Could you let me out here?' Nagi asked the driver. She paid her fare and stepped out of the car, continuing on foot until she came to a beach.

Sea and sky opened out before her – only they weren't blue, but monochrome. The landscape, along with all the buildings and people she had seen on the way there – everything had lost its colour, as though she were living in a black-and-white film.

It hadn't always been like this for Nagi. Something had happened to her vision after that pronouncement from her doctor:

Five years left to live. Written down, it was just five short words. So weighty, yet they hardly took up any space on the page.

Nagi's illness had come on suddenly. At seventeen, reading a book in the library at high school, she had collapsed without warning. Her chest had been in agony, as though it were being crushed, and she couldn't breathe.

Someone had called an ambulance and she was taken to hospital, where the doctors examined her heart and lungs and discovered signs of a serious condition. It had meant immediate surgery, which she'd only just survived.

And so from that point on, hospital had become Nagi's life. She couldn't sit her university entrance exams, and over the next three years she had to undergo several further operations. None of them cured her; all she gained each time was another scar.

At twenty, the doctors gave Nagi and her father an estimate of how long she had left.

Nagi's father had been through it all before. 'Just like with Mum,' Nagi spoke quietly, voicing what she knew he must be thinking: some twenty years earlier, Nagi's mother had also been given five years to live. And, sure enough, when the time was up, she had died.

Like Nagi, her lungs and heart had been weak. Nagi didn't know if her mother's condition had any connection with her own, but she did know one thing.

She would be dead in five years.

*

It was mild for December. The sun shone gently, and a pleasant breeze blew in from the sea. The quiet beach was a welcome contrast to the harsh lights of the hospital and the smell of disinfectant, making it feel as if all the time Nagi had spent lying hooked up to tubes was nothing more than a bad dream. But her body was still patterned with surgical scars, and Nagi knew that the next time she had a seizure, she would be admitted to the hospital where her mother had spent her last days.

Trembling now, thinking about her own end, Nagi wanted to run away – only there was nowhere to go. Death would pursue her wherever she went.

Her mother was the only person who would understand how she was feeling. And that was why she had come here, to this restaurant by the sea. 'Where are you, Mum?' Nagi murmured, as she walked along the empty beach. 'Is there really no more pain in the next world? No more sadness?'

There was no answer, and Nagi fell silent as she walked on.

Eventually, a path strewn with seashells came into view, and, at the end of it, a two-storey building. She had been told she would recognise it by its blue-painted walls, but to her eyes they appeared grey.

As she got closer, she heard a young man's voice. 'How do you keep managing to get out? I must have told you a hundred times, you are *not allowed*. If you can't understand that, I will have to lock you up in a cage. You won't even be able to roam around *in*side anymore.'

The man seemed to be admonishing someone, and Nagi was startled by his words. Who, or what, was he planning to cage?

Raising her gaze from the path, she saw him: a young man in spectacles, crouching down in the doorway. It must have been he who had spoken, and yet he seemed to be alone. Beside him was a chalkboard, on which was written:

The Chibineko Kitchen
We serve remembrance meals.

Nagi felt a wave of relief, knowing that she had found the right place. The chalkboard, however, didn't show the restaurant's opening hours, or any sort of menu – only a note:

This restaurant has a cat.

This was accompanied by a drawing of a kitten — not a very good one, but it had heart. And now Nagi saw why the young man was crouching down.

'*Miaow.*'

Next to the chalkboard was a real kitten. Nagi had missed it at first because it was hidden in the board's shadow, and because it was so little — it looked as though it would fit in the palm of her hand.

'What a cutie!' she couldn't help but say as she approached.

Seeing her, the young man stood up hastily and gave a polite bow. 'Please excuse me. I'm Kai Fukuchi.'

Nagi judged that he must be about three or four years older than she was. What with his apron and his clean-cut appearance, he wouldn't have looked out of place working at a stylish cafe in the city. *Have I come to the wrong Chibineko Kitchen?* she wondered, unable to reconcile the pleasant-looking young man in front of her with what she had been told about the restaurant.

'Miss Hayakawa?' said Kai.

'Y—yes,' Nagi replied. So it *was* the right place.

Kai spoke again. 'Please come in, and I will prepare your remembrance meal.'

*

When Nagi was five, her mother had collapsed and, not for the first time, been carried away in an ambulance. She was frequently in and out of hospital because of her seizures, only this time days passed and Nagi's mother didn't come home.

Nagi and her father visited her so many times that Nagi lost count. Sometimes they would find her mother asleep because of her medication, and at other times the doctor wouldn't allow them in. But they never stopped visiting.

Then one day, as Nagi and her father were leaving their house, he said to her, very seriously: 'Make sure you have a proper talk with Mummy today.'

Nagi had seen tears gathering in his eyes, and fear had gripped her. Years later, she could still remember that moment, and how her father's face had begun to blur through her own tears. She had no memory of their journey to the hospital that day; it was all a blank. The next thing she could recall was standing, alone, beside her mother's bed, in a private room just off the main ward.

Her mother was connected to lots of tubes and was heavily medicated, sleeping with an oxygen mask over her face. Nagi hadn't wanted to wake her, so she had stood listening to the sound of her mother's ventilator, gazing through the window at the sea.

She watched an elderly couple walking slowly along the beach, probably husband and wife. Now and then the old lady came to a standstill, resting and taking in the view, while the old man stuck close by her side, as though he was worried about her. Maybe she was also a patient at the hospital.

Nagi was wishing she could be out there, walking along the sand, when she heard a voice murmur her name. Turning hastily, she saw that her mother's eyes were open, and that she had pulled off her oxygen mask.

'Mummy, you have to put it back on!' she said, pressing the button to call the nurse.

But no bell sounded, and no one came running.

What should I do? She's going to die! Nagi almost cried out, terrified. Then she heard her mother's voice again, and calmed down almost instantly.

'It's all right, I'm not going to die. There's no need to cry.'

'Really . . .?'

'Really. I'm not going quite yet. I've got a little bit of time left.'

Nagi hadn't picked up on what her mother's words meant. She felt only relief. *It's going to be all right.*

'Now then, let's have a chat,' her mother said. 'Here, Nagi, sit down.'

'Okay.' Nagi nodded, and sat in the armchair next to the bed. The chair was so big it almost swallowed her up.

'It's been a while since we had a talk, just the two of us,' her mother continued. It was true, Nagi realised. At the hospital, Nagi's father or a nurse was usually in the room, too.

Nagi had taken her father's words to heart, and had come with lots of things to tell her mother. But now that they were alone she didn't know how to begin. So they sat in silence, until her mother began softly: 'I have to make you an apology.'

'Why?' Nagi asked.

'For not being able to stay with you longer. I'm sorry, Nagi.'

Her mother's voice seemed to echo in Nagi's head. She realised that her mother was saying goodbye, but she didn't want to hear it. *Mummy, please don't go! You have to stay with me!* she wanted to scream. She tried to speak, but silent sobs made it impossible, and large tears plopped down onto the floor.

'Don't cry, Nagi.'

'But . . . but I . . .' Nagi began, and could manage no more.

'Nagi, I have something important to tell you. When

you're missing me badly, and you're desperate to see me again, go to the Chibineko Kitchen.'

Her mother's voice came clearly now, but Nagi didn't understand. The Chibineko Kitchen? She didn't know what that was. Before she could ask, her mother went on: 'It's a restaurant in this seaside town.'

She often referred fondly to this place as 'the seaside town'. *The restaurant must be somewhere not far away.*

'They'll cook you something called a remembrance meal,' she said.

'A remembrance meal?' echoed Nagi.

'That's right. And when you eat it, you can talk to someone who's gone.'

Those were her mother's last words. When she had finished speaking, she closed her eyes slowly and never opened them again.

She looked peaceful, as though she had just fallen asleep.

Nagi and her father resumed life at home, carrying the weight of their sadness together. It was lonely without Nagi's mother, but somehow or other they got by, cooking meals together and taking turns to do the laundry and the cleaning. Even after Nagi became ill herself, she did her share.

'It's you that keeps me going, Nagi,' her father told her time and time again. And that was how they lived – just the two of them, looking after each other.

But now those days, too, were ending. *Five years left to live.* And even less time left to spend at home. Nagi thought she would probably see out her final days in hospital, under the influence of sedatives, just like her mother.

But no – not just her final days: she could be in hospital for months, even a year.

Time was running out for Nagi. She wanted to see her mother again, to hear her voice, before it was too late.

There was another reason Nagi had made up her mind to visit the Chibineko Kitchen.

Early one morning, in September, a few months before she received her terminal diagnosis, Nagi had decided to visit her local park.

It was full of Yoshino cherry trees, and in spring the place was bustling with people sitting under the blossom, eating and drinking and talking. But at other times of year it was quiet, especially early on weekday mornings, so Nagi hadn't expected to see anyone there.

She hadn't woken early; she just hadn't slept all night. Whenever she let her thoughts dwell on her future – no chance of university, no chance of even taking a part-time job, let alone any sort of career – her mood sank so low that sleep became impossible.

Her illness had changed everything. She'd had to drop out of school, and she had stopped replying to friends' Line messages, tired of being asked about how she was. Until one day, Nagi had realised that the only people she spoke to were her father and her doctors and nurses. And her father was always so busy, working like a horse to pay for her treatment.

Nagi had wanted people to leave her be, and now that they were doing just that, she felt desperately lonely. Added to this, stuck at home, she spent all her time trapped in such stifling thoughts they made her chest tight, even when she wasn't having a seizure.

Nagi hated feeling like this – which was why she'd come to the park. Although there was no one to talk to here, either, at least there was open space, and trees and . . . a cat.

The black cat that frequented the park looked too healthy to be a stray, and Nagi presumed it must belong to one of the houses nearby. It seemed to be there every time she visited.

Sure enough, just as she reached the park now, she heard a miaow.

It was the black cat all right, but Nagi was a little surprised to hear it. It didn't normally mew before it had seen her; usually she had to talk to it first, and then, eventually, as though it were an awful bother, the cat would deign to reply. Nagi hoped it wasn't in trouble: being attacked by a crow, perhaps, or being mistreated by someone. That wasn't impossible, although the mew had sounded too nonchalant for that.

Confused, Nagi looked around and then spotted her feline acquaintance. The cat was sitting beside a bench – and it wasn't the park's only occupant. On the bench was a man who looked to be in his late twenties. An easel stood in front of him, and he seemed to be drawing. Neither he nor the black cat noticed Nagi's arrival.

'Stay still,' the man ordered the cat. Nagi realised he was sketching it.

'*Miaow,*' the cat replied, as though the whole experience were too much effort.

'And stop moving your mouth,' said the man. He seemed to be serious, but what an absurd instruction to give a cat!

14

'*Miaow.*' The cat mewed lazily, and curled up on the spot.

The man began to entreat the creature: 'Hey, come on. Please!'

The scene was so ridiculous that Nagi started to laugh, but it came out a little too loudly – man and cat both turned to look at her.

There was a silence. Nagi felt awkward, as though she'd been caught spying on them. She tried to smooth things over, calling out a 'Good morning!'

'Good morning,' the man replied.

And that was how Nagi met Toshiya Nakamori.

With the ice broken, she found that conversation came easily. 'Are you drawing?'

'Yes.' He didn't seem to mind the interruption. He was an artist, he told her. But, struggling to make a living through his art alone, he had a second job to make ends meet.

'But you're so good!' Nagi said, looking at the half-finished picture on Toshiya's canvas.

He hadn't given it any colour yet, but his skill was apparent. The drawing was true to life, almost like a photograph.

'Oh, the world's full of people who can draw like this,' Toshiya said.

The black cat *miaow*ed as though it agreed.

'Why, you . . .!' Toshiya grumbled, and Nagi laughed again.

She hadn't laughed like this for a long time.

From then on, Nagi met Toshiya almost every day. First thing every morning, she would go to the park and there he would be. Sometimes she found him drawing and sometimes he was just sitting, gazing at the cat or the trees.

Nagi learned that he had recently moved to the area and that visiting the park had become part of his daily routine.

'I like it here. It's quiet,' he said.

'Yes. Plus, there's the cat.'

'Right. It doesn't have the temperament to be an artist's model, though.'

'Hey, it's just a bit shy,' Nagi said.

'I don't think so – I think it likes making a fool of me.'

'Surely not!'

These easy exchanges brought a splash of colour into Nagi's life, and she started to look forward to seeing Toshiya.

*

Two weeks after they had first met, Toshiya invited Nagi out. 'Would you like to go for something to eat? There's a cafe near here that does good breakfasts.'

Nagi found herself unable to reply, the spectre of her illness hovering in her mind. Since first being diagnosed, she had resigned herself to the loss of so many things. School. Work. Friends. Love. If she was honest with herself, she was developing feelings for Toshiya, and she wanted to say yes. But it would be reckless – a normal life wasn't on the cards for her, and she knew she shouldn't allow herself to get any closer to him; that she should be content with just sitting in the park, chatting.

She opened her mouth to say, *I'm sorry*, but was interrupted.

'*Miaow.*' The black cat let out a sleepy yawn. It was curled up on the end of the bench where they were sitting. Looking directly at Toshiya, it mewed languidly again.

It did sound a little as though it were making fun of him.

'Come on, we're in the middle of an important conversation here!' Toshiya protested.

But the cat didn't stay to listen, instead jumping down and trotting off briskly, as though it had better things to do.

Nagi suddenly felt silly for overthinking things. Toshiya was only inviting her to breakfast after all. 'Okay. Let's go and get some food.'

After they'd eaten, Nagi and Toshiya took a stroll around the neighbourhood. They passed lots of people on their way to work and school, and normally Nagi would have felt miserable at being the only one who wasn't going anywhere, but today the walk lifted her spirits.

When they were almost back at the park, Toshiya suddenly stopped. 'Wait a moment. I don't want that cat interrupting me again,' he said, and went on before Nagi had time to get a word in. 'Nagi, would you like to go out with me?'

Nagi had seen this coming, and she felt a thrill, knowing that Toshiya felt the same about her as she did about him. But she couldn't say yes. Now was the time, she realised, to be frank and tell him about her illness. After all, her body was a patchwork of scars, and she didn't know when she might next collapse.

'I actually . . .' The words stuck in her throat. She hadn't anticipated how much courage it would take to tell him.

'You don't want to?' Toshiya asked.

'Of course I want to!' Nagi blurted out. She hadn't intended to reveal her feelings for him, but she couldn't stop herself. 'Of *course* I do. If that's what you want.'

Nagi had meant to break up with Toshiya after a few dates: she would simply stop visiting the park and disappear from his life. It had seemed the best thing to do, but she came to realise she'd been thinking only of herself, never considering how Toshiya might feel.

Perhaps what happened next was punishment from the gods for her selfishness.

A few dates later, she and Toshiya were on the way back from a visit to the aquarium when she collapsed on the station platform. They had been standing hand in hand waiting for the train, talking away about something trivial – how they wanted to go for an ice cream or something – and it had happened without warning. Just as the train pulled in, Nagi blacked out, the world growing distant as she sank into darkness.

An ambulance rushed her to hospital, where she underwent surgery again. Toshiya stayed by her side, making no move to go home even as the night wore on. He seemed to think it was his fault she had collapsed; when Nagi came round from the anaesthetic to find her father there, he told her that Toshiya had apologised to him.

'It's my fault, I'm sorry. I shouldn't have taken her traipsing around all those places,' he had said.

'I didn't say anything to him about your illness,' Nagi's father told her.

Toshiya had gone home none the wiser, and if that had been the end of it, perhaps Nagi would have continued seeing him. Her collapse hadn't even hurt this time, unlike in the past, and so Nagi thought it was nothing to worry about. *A little anaemia, maybe.*

But a few days after her surgery, the doctor had come into her room, his brow furrowed, and given Nagi her prognosis.

Five years left to live.

He must have spent time deliberating whether or not to tell her, but death was an almost daily occurrence at the hospital, nothing out of the ordinary.

And now it was coming for Nagi, too.

Nagi's father seemed to have already been given the news: he sat, stony-faced, while the doctor spoke, looking as though he was trying to hold back tears.

Nagi was lost for words; she just sat there in a daze.

'We'll continue with treatment. We won't give up,' the doctor said, but Nagi knew there was little hope.

Despair welled inside her. 'Can you leave me, please?' she said.

Alone, Nagi wanted to cry, but there was something she knew she had to do first. Picking up her phone, she rang Toshiya before her willpower deserted her.

'Nagi—!' he answered straight away, his voice loud with relief; he must have been waiting for her to call.

Nagi found herself wanting to stay on the phone for ever, just listening to him speak. But she knew there could be no more secrets. Their relationship was over. 'I'm sorry for not telling you this before, but I'm ill, and it's really serious. They've told me I only have five years left to live. I'm dying.' Her words came out in a rush. And then she said, 'Goodbye, Toshiya. Thank you for everything.'

Nagi hung up, not waiting to hear his reply. She switched off her phone, and then bawled like a child.

She would never see him again – or so Nagi thought. But the very next day, Toshiya arrived at the hospital.

'Should I ask him to leave?' her father said. His eyes were red and puffy and his cheeks hollow; it was obvious he hadn't slept. The diagnosis had hit him hard: first he had lost his wife, and now he was losing his daughter.

Not wanting to make him act as a go-between, Nagi replied, 'It's fine. I'll tell him myself.' She hated making

21

things difficult for her father, and besides, it was embarrassing.

As soon as her father had left the room, giving her some space, Nagi heard a knock. She took a deep breath.

'Come in.'

The door opened and Toshiya entered.

Nagi looked at him in surprise. She braced herself to tell him again that it was over, but instead found herself saying, 'What's going on? Why are you dressed like that?'

Toshiya was wearing a navy-blue suit. She'd never seen him dressed up like this, as if he were going to a job interview, and it didn't look right on him. At all.

He didn't answer Nagi's question, but said, a serious expression on his face: 'Nagi, I know that your illness is difficult to treat . . .'

It's not just difficult, it's ninety-nine per cent impossible, Nagi was about to point out to him, but before she could open her mouth, Toshiya spoke again.

'Will you marry me?'

For a moment, Nagi couldn't understand what he had said. And then the words sank in. Toshiya was proposing to her.

'You're joking, aren't you . . .?' was all she could manage.

Toshiya shook his head. 'I want to marry you, Nagi.'

'But . . . I'm *dying*.'

Nagi had been keeping a tight lid on her feelings, but now they threatened to burst out anyway. She desperately wanted to say yes, to be with Toshiya for ever. But she also knew that if she really loved him, she could never let him know.

'Please, go home,' she said. She was working so hard to control herself that her voice came out sounding cold. *Well, that can only help.* 'I'm not going to marry you,' she said, in the same flat tone.

How could she marry Toshiya – how could she marry anyone?

'Don't come back again,' Nagi went on. 'I don't want to see you. I never liked you like that anyway.'

'Nagi, listen to me . . .'

'No! Just leave me alone!' she shouted, and then the nurse came in and asked Toshiya to go.

Obediently he did so. And perhaps it was only her imagination, but Nagi thought he looked almost relieved to have been chased away.

Alone, she let her tears fall. *It's better this way*, she told herself over and over. She was grateful to Toshiya. He had given her so many memories – more than enough for someone who only had a few years left. She thought of those early morning chats in the park, the way he had taken her on dates, held her hand, even donned a suit to propose to her. She'd been given the chance to fall in love like a normal girl. It was enough. It really was.

And yet Nagi's tears wouldn't stop. She could hear his footsteps in the corridor, growing fainter, and she pictured him walking away. She could see herself too, laughing as she walked beside him, the way she'd been before her diagnosis.

Eventually the footsteps faded, and Toshiya was gone.

'Goodbye,' Nagi murmured.

The instant she said it, the colour drained from her vision, departing from her life along with Toshiya. One moment everything had looked normal, and the next the world had faded to monochrome.

Nagi supposed it was her condition affecting her eyes. Some patients lost their sight altogether, she knew. She didn't tell anyone her world had turned to black and white. If the hospital staff found out, they'd put her through countless tests, and she didn't want to spend her little remaining time that way. She would rather die like this, she decided, in a black-and-white world. *I'm ready*, she told herself desperately – because if she didn't, the fear would paralyse her.

At the little restaurant by the sea, Kai showed Nagi to a table by the window.

'Will this be all right for you?'

There was no one else in the Chibineko Kitchen – just Nagi and Kai, and the kitten, who was called Chibi.

'Please do accept my apologies,' said the restaurant's young owner. He explained that he was short-staffed that day; ordinarily, there was a girl working there, and when a customer visited for a remembrance meal she would go and meet them off the bus.

'That's okay,' Nagi replied. She had always planned to come by taxi, and besides, she was glad to be spared the inevitable, ugly pang of jealousy she would feel meeting some normal, healthy girl.

Anyway, all that mattered was whether or not she would be able to see her mother. But before Nagi could bring up the subject, Kai continued: 'Please take a seat. I will bring your remembrance meal out shortly.' And he disappeared into the kitchen.

Nagi was left alone with only the kitten for company. With nothing to do as she sat there, her mind began straying – as it all too often did – to thoughts like, *What will happen after I die?* It wasn't the first time she had pictured her own funeral; it even featured in her dreams – her father, sitting there in shock in front of her photograph.

Nagi began to tremble, and a cry began to rise in her throat. *Stop that, it won't help.* To distract herself, she looked around for the kitten and spotted him curled up on a rocking chair by the wall. Next to him was an old grandfather clock; she could hear it – *tick-tock, tick-tock* – steadily marking the time. Looking at the clock was a mistake, Nagi realised. Instead of chasing away her dark thoughts, it intensified them, the ticking of the pendulum sounding like a countdown to death.

I don't want to die! Finally, Nagi let the thought in, and it seemed to reverberate throughout her entire being. *Why me? People live to be a hundred nowadays – why do I have to go at twenty-five?* She just couldn't make sense of it, and she felt the prickle of tears.

Just then, Kai returned, and Nagi hastily rubbed her eyes, blinking the tears away. He was carrying two helpings of food: one for Nagi, the other presumably for her mother.

He placed them on the table. 'Tofu marinated in miso,' he said.

And the moment Nagi looked down at the meal, she pictured her mother's face.

Tofu and miso – both are made from soybeans, and are rich in protein, vitamins and minerals.

'So we all live a little bit longer. Mummy and Daddy, and you too, sweetheart,' Nagi's mother used to say when she cooked tofu at home. She always made sure the family ate healthily.

Of all the dishes she used to cook, it was miso-marinated tofu that Nagi's mother had liked best. It was versatile: the miso meant it paired well with rice, but it also worked as a small side dish, adding a bit of variety to a meal, and it was even good on bread. It wasn't difficult to prepare, either. You just squeezed the water out of the tofu and then marinated it in miso, mirin, soy sauce and sugar, leaving it in the fridge for a day or two.

Now Nagi found that exact dish in front of her once more, prepared for her by Kai.

'Itadakimasu,' she said, putting her palms together neatly before starting to eat.

The miso had a gentle flavour, its richness tempered by the mirin, the salty and sweet elements blending together on her tongue. The texture was just as

27

exquisite; biting down, she found the tofu was soft and creamy like cheese, only lighter.

'The tofu and miso are made with Koitozairai soybeans,' Kai said, explaining that they were cultivated locally, around the Koitogawa River. The name was trademarked, and the beans renowned for their flavour, which made for a sweet tofu and a rich miso.

Nagi recognised the taste. Perhaps her mother had bought tofu and miso made from Koitozairai beans on one of her visits to the seaside hospital? Memories of her mother filled Nagi's head – but that was all. Nothing miraculous occurred. There was no sign of her mother appearing, and neither could Nagi hear her voice.

She sighed and was about to put down her chopsticks when Kai, having returned to the table, said: 'Something more to accompany your tofu.' He placed down a new set of dishes.

'What is it?' Nagi murmured in surprise.

'Onion soup and homemade crackers.'

But it was neither the soup nor the crackers that had caught Nagi's attention; it was the wooden pepper mill that accompanied them.

Kai followed Nagi's gaze. 'Some black pepper for you to season your meal with, if you would like.'

*

Black pepper is made by picking peppercorns – the fruit of the pepper plant – before they are fully ripe, and drying them whole. It is more aromatic and piquant than white pepper, which is made using fully ripe peppercorns with the skins removed.

Pepper always tasted best when it was freshly ground. At Nagi's house they had had a wooden pepper mill, bought by her father, and at mealtimes her parents would turn the mill with a rasping sound and scatter black pepper over their food.

'It goes well on miso-marinated tofu too,' Nagi's mother had always said.

Nagi's parents had liked to eat the marinated tofu on crackers with plenty of black pepper. When Nagi was little, she hadn't liked spicy food, and pepper made her cough; in fact, she had cried the first time she'd tasted it, so her parents never put pepper on her tofu. But she asked for it anyway, wanting to copy her mother and father.

'You're still too little, Nagi,' her mother would say, and then, as though to placate her: 'Tell you what – I'll make it for you when you get a bit bigger.'

'Do you mean it?'

'Of course! And it'll be *much* yummier than what Mummy and Daddy are eating now.'

They'd had this conversation a number of times, the young Nagi eagerly awaiting the day when she would get to taste the promised dish. But before she had been old enough to enjoy the taste of black pepper, her mother had passed away.

'Please take your time.'

Kai went back to the kitchen, leaving Nagi and Chibi alone in the restaurant.

Nagi transferred some of the miso-marinated tofu onto a cracker and ground some black pepper over it. Here was the food she remembered so well, and yet had never tasted. The scent of the pepper cutting sharply across the rich smell of the miso made her stomach rumble and, unable to resist any longer, she took a bite. 'Mmm . . .'

The sound was one of appreciation. The full-bodied flavour of the soft tofu in its miso marinade, the appetising sweetness of the cracker, the kick from the black pepper: everything was perfectly balanced. Though she had never eaten the tofu quite like this before, the taste was achingly familiar and, in an instant, Nagi had polished off the first cracker.

As she reached for a second, she began to cough. She was supposed to be a grown-up now, and yet she was choking on the pepper the same way she had as a child! *It's like nothing's changed at all*, she thought with bitter amusement, as she took a sip of the hot onion soup to calm her throat.

As the steam hit her face she closed her eyes, just for a moment, and when she opened them again she heard a cat mewing.

'*Miaow.*'

It must be Chibi, but he sounded odd somehow. Sort of indistinct.

'What's wrong, kitty? Oh—' Nagi's own voice came out muffled too. She began to feel anxious: was this some symptom of her condition? A sign of an oncoming attack? Given her prognosis, she wouldn't be surprised by anything her illness decided to throw at her.

Fearing she might be about to collapse, Nagi called out for Kai. 'Excuse me! Could you come back in here?'

There was no reply.

'Kai? Mr Fukuchi?' she called desperately, but still not a whisper came from the kitchen. In fact, the whole world seemed to have fallen silent. Nagi could no longer hear the gulls, though they had been crying only moments before, and the breeze had dropped, too.

She looked at the old clock, as though seeking help, and saw that its pendulum had stopped mid-swing. 'What's going on?'

Turning to the window, she received such a shock she thought her heart would seize up there and then. Outside, the waves had ceased all movement. They were frozen in place, as though someone had pressed the pause button.

'What is this . . .? Am I . . .?'

She must be experiencing delirium. Confusion and hallucinations, Nagi knew, weren't so rare among the sick – those suffering from alcohol or morphine addiction, brain disease, exhaustion, even old age. Nagi had heard of people seeing things that weren't there – buildings that had been demolished years before, or the school they used to attend in childhood.

'What do I do?' she cried aloud, bewildered.

At that moment she heard another mew, and remembered that she wasn't alone. She turned to the rocking chair as though Chibi were her last hope, and saw that the little kitten was looking in the direction of the restaurant door.

'Is someone there?'

As though in answer to her question, the door swung open.

A mist seemed to have sprung up from nowhere, and Nagi couldn't see outside the building – it was as though the restaurant were inside a cloud.

And then the hazy figure of a woman appeared through the fog. Nagi couldn't make out her face.

The woman paused in the doorway for a moment as though checking it was the right place, and then stepped inside.

Nagi was speechless. She could only sit and stare as the figure approached her table.

But when the woman spoke, Nagi knew her voice. 'It's good to see you again, Nagi.' And at that moment, her face resolved into one Nagi knew as well as her own.

'Mum . . . it's you.'

The woman standing before Nagi was young; she looked as though she could be in her twenties. *Of course*, Nagi thought. *Mum was just twenty-five when she had me.* Even if she was appearing to Nagi as she had been the last time she had seen her, she would only be thirty.

'May I sit with you?' Her mother indicated the chair opposite Nagi, where her portion of the remembrance meal had been placed.

'Yes,' Nagi murmured, feeling as if she were under a spell.

Her mother sat down. As though letting Nagi in on a secret, she continued: 'Now, I can only stay with you until the food stops steaming.'

'Until it stops steaming?'

'That's right. Once the remembrance meal is cold, I have to return to where I came from.'

So their time together was limited. Nagi cast her gaze down at the food. Only the onion soup was steaming, and it looked as though it was already starting to cool.

Nagi still couldn't quite believe it. Her mother was here, really here! And yet soon she would be gone again.

'Mum, can I talk to you about something?' Nagi said, forcing out the words.

'Of course,' her mother replied – just as Nagi had expected. No matter how busy her mother had been, even towards the end when she'd been bedridden, she had always made time to listen to her daughter. She had always been on Nagi's side.

Nagi knew she would be able to talk to her mother about what was troubling her; that her mother was, in fact, the only person she could tell. So she didn't make any small talk, just said, abruptly: 'I only have five years left to live,' going on to explain that she had contracted a disease of the heart and lungs and been given a terminal diagnosis.

Her mother waited, without interrupting, as if she knew there was more to come.

'And then I fell in love with someone. But I told him to leave me,' Nagi ended, averting her eyes from her mother's gaze.

Nagi knew she had had no choice but to break up with Toshiya. She didn't want to burden him. And if she had joined her life to his, it would only have made her approaching death more painful. Things would be easier if she had nothing important to hold on to. She had been so sure of it. And yet . . . part of her regretted sending Toshiya away. Part of her wished she could be with him until her final moments.

Nagi realised she wanted her mother to reassure her that she had made the right choice. If her fate was inescapable, she would rather resign herself to it. She couldn't bear the thought of any more sorrow.

She had come to the Chibineko Kitchen hoping her mother's words would bring her some peace.

'It was for the best, wasn't it? I was right to break up with him,' Nagi said.

'No,' her mother replied, without hesitation. 'You made the wrong decision.'

Nagi was shocked by her bluntness. 'What do you mean?'

'Well, you're unhappy, aren't you, Nagi? You didn't want to break up with him.'

'Yes, but I . . . I've only got five years left! What would be the point of getting married?' Nagi said, tears forming once more in her eyes.

Nagi had been so sure her mother would understand, would tell her she was right to let Toshiya go. But while Nagi had been relying on her mother to free her of her regrets, instead she was being told she'd made a terrible mistake.

It was the worst thing her mother could have said – Nagi felt as though she had been slapped. She sat there speechless, not even trying to hold back the tears that now streamed down her face.

'You see, it's not *just five years*,' her mother said.

'What do you mean?'

'The time I spent with you was five years too, you know,' her mother went on gently.

Nagi caught her breath. Her mother was right.

'Only five years, but I got to spend them with you, Nagi. I was so glad I had you.'

'Even though you died so soon after?'

Her mother smiled. 'There are lots of ways to measure happiness. Those five years with you gave me more joy than I would have had in fifty years without you.'

Fifty years without me . . .

Oh, no . . .

Nagi began to shake, her mother's words sparking a sudden dread. All this time, and it had never occurred to her. 'Mum, was it . . . was it because of me that you died so young?' Why was she only seeing it now? Giving birth must have put a terrible strain on her mother.

But Nagi's mother shook her head. 'It wasn't your fault, Nagi. It wasn't because I had you. It was because I was ill.'

'But . . . but if you'd never had me, would you have lived longer?'

Though her mother didn't reply, her silence was answer enough.

'Then why would you . . .?' Nagi's voice trembled violently.

'I gave birth to you because it was what I wanted to do,' her mother replied, simply.

'But you must regret it! You must wish you'd never had me!' How could she not? If Nagi hadn't been born, maybe her mother would still be alive.

'Of course not! I knew I wouldn't get to see you grow up, but I never *once* wished I hadn't had you,' her mother replied.

'But—' Nagi began, and her mother interrupted.

'What about you? Do you wish you'd never been born?'

Nagi had, in fact, wished this – over and over again: when she first got ill; when she had to drop out of school; every time she underwent painful procedures; when she was told her condition was incurable.

When she had ended things with Toshiya.

Being alive *hurt*. Living through each day, that count-down ticking in her ears all the while, hurt so much. And yet . . . if she'd never been born, she would never have spent those loving, childhood days with her parents. She would never have met Toshiya, or gone out on dates with him, or been proposed to.

'No. That's not what I wish.' Nagi had lost so much to her illness, and the thought of being robbed of these things, too, was more than she could bear.

'I'm sure Toshiya feels the same way.' Her mother's soft voice enfolded her. 'Meeting someone you love – it's the beginning of such a wonderful time.'

Nagi's memories with Toshiya glowed like jewels in her mind. She wanted to marry him, to grow old with him. She wanted more of those golden, precious moments.

But she had to face the painful reality that they would never grow old together.

'How can I marry him, knowing I'll be dead in five years?' Large tears spilled onto the table. Nagi could hear them fall: *plip, plip, plip.*

Her father had never seemed to know what to do in the face of her tears, but her mother wasn't fazed. 'You're not dead yet, are you?' she said firmly, her tone enough to squash any self-pity.

'N—no, but . . .'

'Well, then,' her mother continued. 'You keep fighting. Don't give in. You're not alone – you've got your father, you've got the doctors and nurses. You must trust the people who're trying to help you.'

Nagi could see so many faces in her mind. Everyone at the hospital who had done so much for her. Her doctor was assiduous, sending away for literature and drugs from overseas to try and tackle Nagi's illness. The nurses were kind, too, indulging her every request. And then there was her father, working from morning until night to pay for her treatment. He must be exhausted, wanting to spit curses at the injustice of it all, and yet he never complained, always having a kind word to spare for his daughter.

'Yes, he really is a catch, isn't he?' Her mother broke into her thoughts, her voice warm. It was obvious she loved Nagi's father, even now.

Nagi could hear Toshiya's voice in her mind. *Will you marry me?*

He had asked, despite knowing full well that her life would be cut short.

It should have been a memory to cherish, yet all Nagi felt now was bitter regret. She loved him, yet she had driven him away. And those words she had hurled at him, those hurtful lies. *I don't want to see you. I never liked you like that anyway.* She desperately wanted to speak to him, to apologise. But it was too late – surely she had squandered whatever affection Toshiya had held for her.

She began to cry once more. Clenching her teeth, Nagi wiped her eyes again and again but the tears kept coming until, giving in, she covered her face with both hands and sobbed.

Nagi's mother, however, wouldn't allow her tears. 'Now, you don't get to decide everything,' she said, speaking to Nagi coaxingly, as though she were still a child.

Nagi didn't understand what she meant. Lifting her face from her hands she looked at her mother, who raised her eyebrows and smiled. 'It's Toshiya who gets to choose whether or not to forgive you. Don't just assume it's too late – go and apologise. Tell him the truth about how you feel.'

Nagi realised her mother was right. She had hurt Toshiya and she knew he might not forgive her. He might not even want to see her. But so be it. It was her turn to admit to her feelings.

'*Miaow.*' Chibi mewed suddenly, as though trying to alert Nagi to something, and she realised that the onion soup was barely steaming. The little kitten was telling her that the miracle was coming to an end.

'I have to go now.'

Nagi's mother stood. Her figure was hazy again, beginning to fade along with the steam from the remembrance meal.

Nagi didn't try and stop her. Somehow, she knew it would be no use.

Her mother walked towards the door, and then she paused and turned to the kitten.

'Thank you for the meal. It was delicious.'

The food at her mother's place was untouched, but to Nagi it sounded as though her mother had really meant it. Nagi had heard the dead ate only by smell; it was why you lit incense for them at their gravesides and the butsudan. It must have been the soup's steam that her mother had enjoyed.

'*Miaow*,' Chibi replied, puffing himself up as though proud of how well the food had turned out.

Nagi's mother smiled, and then she turned to Nagi one last time. 'Isn't it a lovely place?'

'It is,' Nagi replied.

'Bring your dad along next time. He'd like it.'

'I will.' As Nagi nodded, new tears rolled down her cheeks and fell into her remembrance meal. Still she made no move to wipe them away, just keeping her eyes on her mother as though imprinting her in her memory. Her figure was becoming harder to make out.

'Goodbye, Mum.'

'Goodbye, Nagi.'

'I'm glad you had me,' said Nagi, meaning every word.

'And I'm glad you were born.'

Her mother smiled, and Nagi laughed. It wasn't as if she felt no sorrow – but there was a new lightness there, too.

'Bye now, Nagi.'

'Bye.' Nagi nodded once more as her mother faded

away. She could hear her footsteps, and then the door to the restaurant opened and closed.

'Thank you, Mum,' Nagi whispered after her.

The frozen scene came to life once more: the pendulum of the old clock resumed its swing; the sound of waves drifted in from outside; and the black-tailed gulls called, *miaoow, miaoow*. Nagi felt as though she had awoken from a dream.

'She's gone . . .' she murmured.

'*Miaow*,' Chibi replied. The kitten's voice was no longer muted: he had accompanied Nagi back to the ordinary world.

Kai came out of the kitchen carrying a tray with two teacups on it. From one of them wafted a pleasantly toasty scent. 'Some barley tea for you.'

He must have selected it with Nagi's health in mind. Barley tea didn't contain caffeine, and was often served to pregnant women and those who were ill.

From the other cup rose the invigorating smell of green tea.

'This one is Sakura tea,' said Kai.

'Sakura tea?'

'Yes – the leaves are grown in a place called Sakura, not too far from here. It has a nice, deep fragrance and taste.' Kai placed the second cup down next to Nagi and, in response to her questioning look, said: 'We are expecting another customer.'

Someone else must have made a reservation. But why serve the tea before they had even arrived? And why set it down beside her when all the other seats were available?

'With my colleague off today, there's no one to go and greet our guest,' Kai said, meaningfully.

Nagi frowned, puzzled, unsure what this had to do with her – he'd already told her they were short-staffed. Her thoughts were interrupted when she heard Chibi mew again. He was standing on his back legs, stretching up to look out of the window. Seeming to feel Nagi's eyes on him, he looked back at her and mewed a second time.

Was he trying to tell her something? She glanced at the window to see what Chibi was looking at.

'Ah, I believe he's here,' said Kai.

'Who?'

'Our customer.'

Nagi saw him then, and her heart did a somersault. It was Toshiya. He was here, walking towards the Chibineko Kitchen.

And then one more miracle happened.

44

The moment Nagi caught sight of Toshiya, the colour returned to her world. The blue sky and sea, the brilliant white of the gulls and the seashell path – all were vivid and bright. Nagi saw, for the first time, that Chibi the kitten was white with ginger patches. Toshiya, she noticed, was wearing a white tuxedo and carrying a bouquet of red roses.

'What's going on? What's he doing here?' she asked, in a bewildered whisper.

'The reservation was made by a Mr Takashi Hayakawa,' Kai replied, seeing Nagi's confusion.

Nagi's father. So he already knew of the Chibineko Kitchen. She guessed that her mother must have told him about it.

Perhaps Nagi's father, who was always watching over her, had noticed her leaving the house and worked out where she was heading. Maybe he had phoned the restaurant to find out for himself, and then called Toshiya.

But that get-up, and the roses—

Just as Nagi's racing thoughts caught up with the situation, Toshiya spotted her through the window.

'Marry me, Nagi!' he called.

And everything fell into place. The white tuxedo, the red roses – Toshiya was proposing to Nagi for a second time.

'Oh, no, what a cliché!' she murmured to herself. Proposing like this to a girl who didn't have long to live—? It was hackneyed, the stuff of films and TV shows. So absurd as to be laughable.

And yet she was overjoyed. Who cared if it was clichéd, who cared if anyone laughed? She was just glad to see him.

Nagi looked out at Toshiya, these realisations running through her head, and then heard Kai say, gently: 'I do apologise, but would you mind going to greet him?'

'You want me to go out?'

'Yes. I would go myself, but at present I have my hands full—' Nagi saw that it was true: Kai was holding Chibi in his arms. 'If I don't hang on to him he'll get outside, you see,' and the little cat *miaow*ed as though to confirm this. 'I would hate for Mr Nakamori to get lost,' Kai said, his voice innocent, his face serious.

These things did happen. Somehow or other people managed to lose their way, even when the path was right there in front of them. Nagi hesitated, still unsure of her own footing.

'Could you? Or perhaps it's too much to ask?' Kai said, looking as though butter wouldn't melt.

'Of course it's not. I'll fetch him,' Nagi replied. She stood up and headed for the door.

And for Toshiya.

She had things to tell him. She knew that suffering lay ahead, that she might lose the ability to move, to speak, to breathe unassisted, that she might even die resenting Toshiya and her parents and wishing she'd never been born.

And yet . . . it was nothing more than a dream, but it was there: the tantalising thought that she might get better, and that happiness could be hers.

Nagi decided to let hope in. She decided to have faith in the people around her, to have faith in herself. She decided to believe in love. It was far, far better than believing in nothing at all.

I won't run away anymore.

She could smell the sea as she opened the door of the Chibineko Kitchen. Toshiya stood before her.

'Nagi . . .'

Her heart beat wildly and she felt her cheeks flush with happiness. But she knew she could be happier still, and so she answered him, her voice loud and clear: 'Yes, I'll marry you! I love you, Toshiya!'

They were going on a journey, the two of them. No more running away, no more giving up. It was a cruel world, but Nagi wasn't going to turn her back on it.

She would keep on walking until her final moments, her head held high.

A special recipe from the Chibineko Kitchen

Tofu no Misozuke: Miso-marinated tofu

Ingredients (serves 2)
- Approx. 150g firm tofu
- 3–5 tbsp miso paste
- Mirin, soy sauce and sugar – to taste

Method
1. Place a weight on top of the tofu to squeeze the water out of it until the block has lost about half of its thickness.
2. Mix the miso with a little mirin, soy sauce and sugar to form a thick paste.
3. Coat the tofu all over with the miso mixture and wrap it in a sheet of kitchen roll.
4. Wrap the whole thing in cling film or place it in a freezer bag and leave it to marinate in the

fridge for at least one night, but ideally for two days.

5. Scrape the excess miso off the tofu, cut into bite-size pieces and serve.

Tips

We recommend grinding black pepper over the tofu before eating.

2

A black-mask cat and pork belly kara-age

チバザポーク
'Chiba The Pork'

Chiba Prefecture is one of Japan's leading producers of pork, and the various products are marketed under the brand name 'Chiba The Pork'.

Pigs cannot regulate their own body temperatures well, and so one key aspect of pig farming is maintaining a comfortable ambient temperature. The mild climate of Chiba is perfect for this: the prefecture is bordered by the sea on three sides and rivers in the north, and with the Kuroshio current flowing up the east coast of the Boso Peninsula, the summers are cool and the winters warm. These consistent

temperatures are what gives Chiba pork
its delicious taste.

Chiba The Pork

Where had the time gone?

Keita Miyata would be forty next year, and yet here he was, unemployed and living shut away in his room.

It hadn't always been like this. Twenty years ago, after graduating from high school, he had found a job at a local second-hand car dealership. The salary hadn't been bad, but the workload had been tough: despite having asked for an administrative role when he joined the company, Keita had been assigned to the sales team.

'You need to be shifting five cars a month,' he was told on his very first day.

Keita had been given training along with the other new hires, but none of the advice they received seemed particularly helpful. The sessions mostly involved being yelled at.

The new recruits had to do their own yelling, too.

'Sell or go home!' they were made to shout over and over again.

'Think like a customer!'

'Anyone can be persuaded!'

'You're only worth the sales you make!'

If they weren't loud enough, they were yelled at some more and ordered to do press-ups on the spot. Keita hated having to raise his voice, so he spent most of the training sessions on the floor, and left with aching muscles.

He wasn't even taught the basic etiquette for handing over a business card.

Although Keita was desperate to do well, when he was sent out to talk to potential buyers he barely managed to get anyone to hear him out, let alone purchase a car. Days went by and he hadn't managed to close a single sale.

One morning, when he arrived at work, his boss, Ishida, called over to him: 'Hey, you! Shirker!'

At first Keita hadn't realised Ishida was talking to him, and he'd just continued getting set up at his desk. Then—BANG!

Keita nearly jumped out of his skin. Ishida had slammed his hand down on his desk, and Keita looked up to see the man glowering across the room at him.

'Look at me when I'm speaking to you, *shirker*.'

'Sorry . . .' Keita said.

'Why didn't you answer me?'

'I . . . I didn't realise you meant me.'

'Who else would I be talking to? Do you see anyone else slacking off around here?'

'I'm sorry,' Keita said, again. Not brave enough to answer back, all he could do was apologise. He was, after all, the only one of the new hires who hadn't managed to sell a single car.

'Come over here,' said Ishida.

'Y—yes, boss.'

'I can't hear you!'

'Yes, boss!' repeated Keita, and approached Ishida's desk.

'So, when do you plan on coming back to work?' asked Ishida.

'What?' Keita hadn't taken a single day off yet. In fact, he had been working on the evenings and weekends, too. He hadn't expected to be paid for the extra hours, so he hadn't been clocking in and out, but he'd thought Ishida was aware of how much time he spent there. 'I haven't booked any time off,' he said. Keita's voice was timid even to his own ears, but at least he had managed to form a response. He was sure Ishida must be mixing him up with someone else.

'Don't you know sarcasm when you hear it?' Ishida snorted.

At that moment sniggers broke out across the office, and Keita realised everyone was laughing at him.

'You haven't sold a single car! So you might as well be on holiday!'

'I'm sorry . . .'

'Is that all you can say? You think an apology's going to cut it? You don't think this is *funny*, do you?'

'No, of course not.'

'Then get out there and *sell*! I'm not the one you need to bow and scrape to. Save that for the customers!'

'Yes, boss . . .'

' "Yes, boss?" Do you actually understand what I'm saying?' Ishida glared at him. 'What's your plan? Come on, tell me how you're going to get the job done.'

'Er . . . I'll keep at it until I make a sale.'

'No, that's not good enough!'

'What?'

Ishida gave a disgusted sigh. 'Look, you've *been* keeping at it, haven't you? You've been working day in, day out, and you haven't sold a single car.'

Keita nodded.

'So use your head. Do you see what I'm saying?'

'No,' Keita answered truthfully, and Ishida sighed again. Then, lowering his voice, as though letting Keita in on a secret, he said: 'Target customers who are *easy wins.*'

'Easy wins?'

'That's right. There are people who'll listen to you, yes? Your parents, your brother, your sister, your friends – even the kids who were in the years below you at school. *Those* are the people you want to go for.'

It wasn't unheard of for new hires to go selling to relatives or friends. It was the same in any industry, not just used cars. But Keita couldn't do it. He just couldn't.

'I can't,' he replied, his voice barely audible. His mother could never afford a car, even a second-hand one, and he wasn't in touch with any of his other relatives. None of his friends would be likely to buy a car from him, either.

'Useless.' Ishida tutted scornfully. 'It doesn't matter where you work – you'll never get anywhere.'

Keita didn't know what to say. He felt so humiliated, he was sure he'd cry if he opened his mouth.

'All right, I can see it's no use talking about it. Just go back to your desk and take a nap until you get fired,' said Ishida.

'B—but . . .'

'Don't talk to me, I'm busy.' Ishida pointed at the paperwork strewn across his desk. 'Know why that is?

You're a drain on our resources, which means I've got to work extra hard.' But he hadn't finished sticking the knife in. He looked up, and his voice boomed across the office: 'Everyone else is working late. You've all got to make up for this freeloader. Got it?'

'Yes, boss,' came the listless answer, the employees glaring at Keita and sighing loudly.

He couldn't do it anymore. Before the day was out, Keita had handed in his notice. Nobody tried to stop him.

It hadn't even been one month.

And that was the sum total of Keita's employment history. Of course, he had tried hard to find other jobs. He scoured the newspapers for listings and went for interviews, but he was never hired. On several occasions he was told, 'We can't take on someone who's going to quit after a month.' When he explained how awful his previous employer had been, he was met with scornful laughter. Nobody understood; they simply assumed Keita was to blame.

Each time he was rejected, Ishida's words echoed in his mind. *It doesn't matter where you work – you'll never get anywhere.*

His old boss had been right. In fact, his jibe had suggested Keita would at least be working *some*where, but he couldn't even manage that.

Keita found himself starting to shake whenever he thought about attending an interview, the panic attacks getting worse and worse until, one day, he began hyperventilating so badly that he collapsed and had to be taken to hospital.

'Don't overdo it, Keita,' his mother told him.

Keita's parents had divorced when he was in his final year of primary school. Being so young at the time, all he had known about it was that his father had racked up some debts and then left town, and Keita had no reason to doubt this version of events.

Even when his father had been living with them, he was hardly ever home, so Keita didn't miss his dad after he walked out – but it did mean there was never enough money. Up until his father's departure, the family had lived in a modern, spacious flat, but after the divorce Keita and his mother moved to a shabby little low-rise in an out-of-the-way neighbourhood. The place was too cold in winter and too hot in summer, and had only two small rooms, besides the bathroom and the cramped kitchen.

Though they had downsized, there were still bills to be paid, and Keita's mother began work at a rehabilitation centre. It offered care for elderly people who were injured or unwell, looking after them until they could return home.

At first Keita's mother had only worked there part-time, but the centre soon made her a permanent employee. She would often be out all day, and sometimes even stayed overnight, but she was so badly paid that she and Keita only just managed to get by.

Despite these financial worries, Keita's mother never pestered him to get a job. 'I'll do the earning for now. You just take it easy,' she said, and Keita, as much as he wanted to go out and make a living so his mother could put her feet up, did just that.

A growing fear of work overshadowed everything else.

Gradually, Keita had stopped going out. He kept out of his mother's way by only leaving his room to use the bathroom, even timing his meals so that he was eating while she was out at work. He felt pathetic for failing to get a job, and he couldn't look her in the eye.

As long as Keita stayed inside, life was easy. No one could ridicule him or call him a shirker. He stopped checking the job adverts. A year went by, and then two.

Keita's mother continued to look after him: she cleaned, she did the washing, she cooked his meals and left them for him in the kitchen. And she spoke to him from the other side of his bedroom door: 'What would you like to eat? If you want anything special, let me know and I'll go out and get it. Oh, yes, that reminds me – why don't we go for a nice meal on my next day off?'

Her kindness only hammered home to Keita just how pitiful he was; every time he heard her voice he felt a prickle of irritation, and he wished she would leave him alone. What good would it do to go outside now, after all this time? It would only remind him of everything he had missed out on.

Sometimes, in lieu of a reply, Keita would bang his fist against the wall. The shame he felt after these outbursts made it even harder to face his mother.

Day after useless day went by, Keita brooding on how, if his life had been a film, it would be high time for some dramatic turn of events. But this was reality, and instead, one month blurred into the next, until he lost track of time all together.

And then suddenly he was approaching forty, still unemployed, still a recluse. It was cruel how little had happened in all those years.

His mother was in her sixties now – past retirement age, Keita thought. But still she went out to work, after cooking his meals and speaking to him through his door.

Keita never asked himself how many more years this could go on for: he had come to take it for granted now, that his mother would provide for him. He could live without having to work – or so he thought.

One morning, Keita's mother didn't come to his door. He waited until the time when she usually headed out to work, but he didn't hear her leave. He wondered if she had the day off but, even so, he was surprised not to hear the usual sounds of her cooking and cleaning. Had she slept in? It didn't seem likely. She always woke before her alarm.

'What's going on?' he muttered to himself. Though his mother's presence often irked him, now that there was no sign of her he felt a deep sense of unease creeping over him. His chest grew tight, as though there wasn't enough air. 'Better go and have a look . . .'

The flat was only small, and as soon as he opened his door he heard it: the sound of running water. There was a washbasin in the narrow room that led to the bathroom, and Keita saw that the door was ajar and the lights were on. But he couldn't hear his mother busying herself at the sink.

'Mum?' he called out. There was no reply, only the sound of water, trickling.

Keita's heart began to race, sure something had happened. Something bad.

He peered around the hallway door and froze. His mother was lying on the floor. Water was overflowing from the sink and splashing onto her face, yet she didn't react.

'M—Mum!' Keita finally found his voice, but still his mother didn't respond.

He called an ambulance.

But it was too late. His mother had collapsed while washing her face at the sink. The medics told him that it had been a stroke, and that she was already gone by the time the ambulance had arrived.

It wasn't grief that gripped Keita so much as terror: he had no idea how he was going to survive. When he looked at his bank book to see how much money he had in his account, he realised it was hardly anything – only enough to last a month or two. He pictured himself being evicted from the flat, unable to pay the rent.

If he lost this place, he would be homeless.

'What am I supposed to do . . .?'

*

After the funeral, one of the carers from the rehabilitation centre stopped by the flat to speak to Keita.

'Why don't you come and work with us?' The woman appeared to be somewhere in her early thirties, with short hair and no trace of make-up on her face. She had a steely look about her. She must have heard about him from his mother.

'Guess I could, maybe . . .' Keita mumbled. He did need a job, as soon as possible.

The woman frowned. 'Don't you know how to speak properly? You're nearly forty, aren't you?'

This stung, but Keita didn't have the nerve to get into an argument with a woman he'd only just met. Instead, he corrected himself, saying meekly, 'I'd be very grateful for your help.'

But as soon as the woman had gone, Keita was hit by a nauseating wave of anxiety. His whole body shook, and he was terrified he might start hyperventilating again. He didn't *want* to work. He was afraid to leave the flat.

'I just *can't* . . .' he whispered to himself. He went into his mother's room, hoping he might find some money or another bank book. He had already checked her chest of drawers and the desk, but he hadn't had a proper look through her cupboard yet, and now he slid open the door.

There was no money in there, but on the top shelf he found a long, thin parcel. It was neatly gift-wrapped, the paper bearing the name of a smart department store that even Keita had heard of.

He picked it up and saw there was a small card attached.

'To Keita,' was all it said. The writing was his mother's. The wrapping paper still looked crisp and there was no trace of dust on it; the parcel couldn't have been there for more than a year.

'What's this?' Keita muttered, a puzzled frown on his face as he unwrapped the box.

Inside was a simple navy-blue tie.

Keita almost cried. Though he had barely left his room for the past twenty years, his mother had never given up on him. She had believed that the day would come when he would go back out into the world.

Nor was it all he found in the cupboard. There were more gift-wrapped boxes, and paper bags. He opened them to discover handkerchiefs and smart shirts, socks, underwear, a fountain pen, a nice ball-point pen . . . There were twenty presents in total. She must have bought him something every year. Twenty years' worth of her hopes for her son had been stowed away on the top shelf of the cupboard.

Keita fell to his knees in his mother's room and cried his eyes out. 'Mum, I'm so sorry . . .' he sobbed through his tears.

The next day, Keita put on the tie and went out to work. His shirt, his socks, even the underwear he was wearing, had all come from the top shelf of the cupboard.

The woman who had spoken to him after his mother's funeral was called Shiori Ejiri. She was thirty-four years old, and she had started working at the rehabilitation centre fifteen years earlier, shortly after finishing high school. As people didn't tend to stay long in the care profession, Shiori was indisputably an old hand. Many of the staff even called her 'boss'.

'Just think of me as the site supervisor,' she explained to Keita. She had dropped all polite forms of speech with him now, despite being five years his junior.

Keita had joined the team as a part-time worker and been told to follow Shiori's instructions. But she didn't seem inclined to give him much guidance. 'Just keep out from under my feet, and don't bother the other staff. Everyone has their hands full, we don't have time to run around looking after you too.' Having delivered this command, she bustled off, called away by someone.

And so Keita, still utterly clueless, started work.

The centre – an imposing five-storey building – had been completely rebuilt the year before, and as a result was clean and modern. Some of the patients were resident at the home, but the facility also acted as a day centre, and there was a constant stream of elderly people and their carers coming and going.

The staff hurried about, ignoring Keita. Though he wasn't itching to work, exactly, he felt ill at ease standing doing nothing. Catching hold of Shiori when she next happened to pass by, he asked her what he should do.

'I told you, just keep out of the way,' was her brusque reply.

'B—but . . .'

'Well, what can you do?' she asked.

'I mean, I—' Keita faltered.

'*Can* you do anything?'

'No . . .' he conceded, dropping his gaze. He had been shut away for twenty years, and now he was capable of nothing.

It doesn't matter where you work – you'll never get anywhere. The words rang once again in Keita's ears, and he felt a desperate urge to run for the safety of his room. It had been hard enough dragging himself this far and now,

66

despite the courage his mother's gifts had given him, it looked as though he was going to fail this time too.

His eyes smarted with tears and his body began to tremble. Shiori, appraising him coolly, said, 'Don't make that face.'

'What? What do you mean?' Keita, taken aback by her remark, stopped shaking.

'Our job here is to look after people. There are no miserable faces allowed, or you'll worry our clients.'

Maybe she had a point. And then this younger woman – his boss – gave him an order. 'I need you to smile. You might have been shut away, but you still know how to do that, don't you?'

Keita wasn't sure that he did. He couldn't even remember the last time he had. 'I can't . . .' he started honestly, and then broke off, realising this was exactly what he had said to the boss at his old company twenty years before.

It was going to happen all over again: the disappointment, the ridicule.

Keita braced himself, but Shiori didn't sneer at him. She just looked thoughtful, and then issued a new instruction.

'Okay, well – could you wear a face mask and do the cleaning, until you can manage to smile? That way your face will be mostly hidden.'

'All right.'

'And one more thing. If any of the clients talk to you, make sure you answer them properly. Speak clearly, in a nice, cheerful voice.'

To Keita this sounded about as impossible as smiling, but for some reason he decided to give it a go. 'I'll try my best,' he said.

'Good. I've got high hopes for you.' Shiori beamed broadly at him, as if setting an example. And while her tone was no-nonsense, her eyes were kind.

Keita's work at the rehabilitation centre didn't involve caring directly for the residents. When he had asked Shiori about this, she'd replied: 'You're just a part-timer, you don't do those tasks yet.' She told him that the first step in becoming a carer was completing the basic training. It involved a forty-hour study course, ninety hours of practical training and a written exam.

'If you want to work here permanently, you need to get your certification. Then you'll get a wage increase, too,' Shiori said.

The benefits of a full-time role were appealing, but still Keita hesitated: he could see the work would be tougher than he had initially imagined. Helping clients eat and drink, use the toilet, and bathe: these were the three key components of personal care. At the moment, his only task was cleaning – but that was no walk in the park, either. Some of the centre's clients had dementia, others physical impairments. They would spill their food, and some didn't always make it to the toilet in time. If Keita didn't clean up quickly, he would get a scolding from Shiori. And she wasn't shy about telling him off in front of the clients or the other staff.

'Come on, clean it up properly!'

'Quickly! Are you even trying?'

'Do you call that cleaning? Don't you know how to use a mop?'

But Keita felt this was fair enough. If he did a sloppy job cleaning the floors, someone could slip and fall – and for an elderly person, that could be fatal.

However, there were some of Shiori's reprimands that didn't make sense to him. Like the time she berated him for taking a client's hand to guide him to the toilet.

'What are you doing? If you coddle the clients, they won't be able to fend for themselves anymore!'

'But . . . it's just, he couldn't even walk straight,' Keita said.

The old man Keita had led to the toilet had just had a major operation. Surely a fall *now* of all times would be especially serious.

But Shiori shook her head. 'The point of the rehabilitation centre is to get people back into their own homes. You mustn't over-nurse them.'

In fact, Keita had been cautioned about this several times. But the line between nursing and *over*-nursing was blurry, and besides, he had no experience. How was he supposed to know?

These thoughts must have registered on his face, because Shiori glared at him. 'You're not even trying to understand, are you? Maybe you're not right for this work after all. If you don't want to do the job, then just quit now.'

It was an awful thing to say to him. Why couldn't she see that he was doing the best he could?

Fine then, I will! he thought. *I'll quit right now, if that's what you want.* He hadn't even asked for the job in the first place. He would go along to the job centre tomorrow and find something else. Shiori had pushed him around for the last time.

A year had passed, and Keita had turned forty.

It was a weekday morning, but he wasn't on his way to work. Instead, he was riding a Sobu Line rapid train bound for a town on the coast. The train did have a first-class section, a double-decker carriage mainly occupied by commuters, but Keita was standing in one of the regular carriages. He had been reluctant to part with the extra fee to guarantee himself a seat for the journey. In fact even buying a standard class ticket stung – but there was somewhere he wanted to go.

The restaurant by the sea in Uchibo. The Chibineko Kitchen.

Keita couldn't remember when or where he had first heard of the place – perhaps it was his mother who had told him about it. But somehow the restaurant's name and location had lodged themselves in the recesses of his mind and, one day, the place had just popped into his head.

He had decided to look it up online, and had come across a blog that had hardly any views. It was written by the woman who owned the restaurant. She seemed to be using the blog as a journal, posting about this and that.

Keita learned that the woman's husband had disappeared one day when he had gone out to sea to fish, and that she had begun making kagezen meals to pray for his safety. Word had spread, and her customers had started to request kagezen too, in memory of family and friends who had died. The woman had called these 'remembrance meals'.

'And then a miracle happened,' she wrote. 'Something unbelievable.'

Each time she cooked a remembrance meal, the customer who had ordered it would find memories of their lost loved one flooding back to them. On occasion, customers told her they had heard their dead friend or relative speak; some even said they had appeared in front of them.

Keita found it hard to believe; it had to be one of those urban legends doing the rounds online. And yet he called the Chibineko Kitchen and made a reservation. Despite his doubts, he found himself drawn to the place.

It had been a year since his mother's death, and he needed to speak to her. He couldn't be happy until he had seen her. There was something he desperately wanted her to know.

The train arrived at the seaside town, and Keita left the station and boarded a bus.

The voice on the other end of the phone had offered to send someone to meet him at the bus stop, but Keita had declined. The journey was straightforward, and he didn't want to put the restaurant staff to any trouble. Besides, he felt he would like to walk the last part alone.

The bus was almost empty. The only other passenger was an elderly woman who must have been at least eighty. She wore an elegant kimono and appeared well-to-do.

Money makes all the difference in life, Keita thought, enviously. He wouldn't have had to take the job at the rehabilitation centre if he'd been rich.

The stop buzzer sounded, the bus came to a halt and the old lady got up to make her way to the door. It seemed an odd place to be getting off. They had stopped in a desolate spot and all Keita could see was a disused factory; there didn't appear to be any houses nearby.

The old lady had an air of vulnerability about her, her hands shaking as she struggled to get the change out of her purse. It was a plump purse, too – she probably had a wad of ten-thousand-yen notes in there.

She managed to extricate her fare and hand it to the driver, before getting off the bus. But she didn't put her purse back in her bag, instead keeping it clutched in one hand.

'Excuse me! I'm getting off here too!' Keita called to the driver.

*

Kotoko Niki looked over at the Chibineko Kitchen's old clock. Almost 11 a.m.

An hour had gone by and there was still no sign of Keita Miyata. He hadn't even called to say he'd be late for his reservation. Kotoko had started working part-time at the restaurant earlier that month, but she had been there long enough to know that it wasn't looking promising.

'Do you think he's coming?'

'I'm not sure,' Kai replied quietly. 'I apologise for keeping you here with nothing to do, but would you mind if we waited a little longer?'

He spoke so politely, just as he had when they first met. He never dropped the habit. Kotoko almost sighed out loud. It wasn't as though they were a couple or anything – they were just colleagues, so it was only natural for there to be some distance between them, but she did wish he would speak to her a little less formally.

Not as though we're a couple. Kotoko's cheeks reddened at the thought. She was all over the place today. This was what happened when you had too much time on your hands. The restaurant wasn't open to other diners on days when they had a booking for a remembrance meal, so there was no other work to be getting on with.

And since they only ever opened for breakfast, it wasn't as though there were things to get ready for the afternoon.

The Chibineko Kitchen's unusual opening hours were a hangover from the time Kai had been closing early so that he could go and visit his mother in hospital.

Kotoko knew all about that.

By the time Nanami's cancer had been discovered, it had spread through her body and become inoperable. When she was hospitalised, it was not to treat the illness but to relieve the pain. She had entrusted her glasses to Kai then, saying *When I get better and come home, I'll want to do lots of reading.* Kai had known that she had intended them as a keepsake for when she was gone. But still he had prayed his mother would recover.

There had been no miracle in the end, however, and Nanami had died. Kai and Chibi had said their goodbyes, and then Kai had gone alone to the crematorium – he couldn't take the little cat with him, of course – where he had gathered his mother's bones from the ashes and placed them in an urn, along with her glasses. He had never really believed in an afterlife, but he had stood there nonetheless, hands pressed together, and offered a prayer for his mother in the next world.

I hope you have everything you need, and all the books your heart desires. I hope you are free of troubles, in that place where there is no sickness.

Now Nanami was at rest in a cemetery on the edge of town. And almost every day, after he had closed the Chibineko Kitchen, Kai went to visit her grave.

'I just wasn't sure about changing the opening hours all of a sudden,' Kai told Kotoko. But he did keep the restaurant open for longer when a customer required it, and it seemed that today would be one of those days.

He's too good-natured, Kotoko thought. She was feeling particularly impatient because there was something she wanted to talk to Kai about once they had finished for the day.

Kotoko had been taking time out from university following the unexpected death of her older brother in an accident, but the year was coming to an end now. If she wanted to resume her studies in the spring she would have to start making arrangements.

And then there was the theatre company. She had only just joined, yet she found herself torn between returning to university, and dropping out and throwing herself into acting, as her brother had done. When she had spoken to her parents about it, they had simply told her that it was her life and her choice, and that she should try and live with no regrets. Kotoko knew her parents would really prefer her to return to university, but they hadn't tried to influence her – perhaps because Yuito's death had brought home to them just how fleeting life could be.

She couldn't make up her mind. Kotoko wanted to stay on at the Chibineko Kitchen, too, but she wasn't confident she could juggle all three commitments. It would be exhausting to keep travelling back and forth between Tokyo and Kimitsu in Chiba Prefecture. And even Yuito – a far more brilliant and capable person than she was – hadn't tried to take on everything at once: he had thought that in order to devote himself to acting, he had better quit university.

As Kotoko mulled this over, another half-hour passed. It was nearly noon now, and almost the end of her shift. She felt guilty about being paid without having done any work, and the restaurant covered her travel costs, too, which weren't cheap.

'Let me go to the bus stop and see if he's there,' she said now. But just as she started for the door, Chibi gave a mew.

'*Miaow.*'

Kotoko got the impression the little cat was telling her to wait. She looked over and saw that both Chibi and Kai were peering out of the window.

'It looks as though he's here.'

Before Kotoko could reply, the door to the Chibineko Kitchen swung open.

'I'm sorry I'm late. I'm Keita Miyata – I had a reservation—?'

The man bowed his head as he stepped into the restaurant. He looked youngish, but his hair, a little on the long side, was flecked with grey. His smart shirt and tie looked somewhat threadbare, as though he'd worn them often.

'Can I still come in?' he asked hurriedly, before Kai and Kotoko had spoken a word of greeting. He seemed worried they would turn him away, which, given how late he was, wasn't surprising.

Kai had told Kotoko Keita's story after he had taken the reservation over the phone: he had lost his mother to a stroke around a year ago, and had called the Chibineko Kitchen because he wanted to see her. Kotoko knew nothing beyond that.

'There's something I want my mother to know.'

Those had been Keita's words, according to Kai. It almost sounded as though Keita might be holding some sort of grudge against his mother.

Had he come all this way to settle a score?

Kotoko noticed that Keita had a canvas bag slung over his shoulder and was clutching the strap tightly. His brow was drenched with sweat.

'Am I too late?' he asked again, a touch of resignation in his voice. Any ordinary restaurant would have cancelled his booking by now.

But the Chibineko Kitchen wasn't any ordinary restaurant.

'No, it's perfectly all right. Please take a seat by the window.'

Kotoko's job was to shop for the ingredients for the restaurant, go out to greet customers, and clean up the kitchen and tables after they'd left. The cooking and serving was all done by Kai, so while there were customers at the restaurant her only real task was to make the tea. She was free to chat with the diners while Kai was preparing their food, but the people who ordered remembrance meals tended to be very quiet, lost in their own thoughts.

On this occasion, however, Keita spoke up. 'Could I charge my phone?' he asked, taking out a charging cable.

A dead battery might explain why he hadn't called.

The Chibineko Kitchen was a fairly old building, and there was only one wall socket, over by the grandfather clock. 'Please feel free,' Kotoko said, pointing it out to Keita.

Chibi sat, as usual, in the nearby rocking chair, looking for all the world as though he owned it. He twitched an ear at this exchange and then let out a *'Miaow,'* as though granting Keita his permission to plug in his phone.

'Oh, great. Thank you,' Keita said to Kotoko.

His phone was quite an old one, she noticed. And the charger looked out of date too – the cable so short it didn't even reach the table.

'Do you mind if I leave it on the chair until it's charged?'

'Go ahead.'

'Thank you.' Keita placed the phone beside Chibi, who peered curiously at the lit-up charging light. He kept his paws to himself, however, and didn't seem inclined to play with it.

Eventually the kitchen door opened, and the aroma of sesame oil filled the room. The meal was ready.

'Thank you for your patience,' Kai said, as he placed dishes of crispy deep-fried meat on the table. It was kara-age, but not made with the usual chicken. 'Here is your remembrance meal. Pork belly kara-age.'

*

Chiba has a long history of pig farming. According to the local government website, there are records dating back to the 1830s of pigs being reared in several villages in Kazusa, an old province located in modern-day Chiba Prefecture. The pigs are fed sweet potatoes, sardine meal, rice bran and by-products from soy-sauce production, making their meat tender and delicious.

This was the pork that Kai had cooked with today: he had cut the thinly sliced belly meat into bite-size pieces and then massaged it in a marinade of saké, soy sauce, grated ginger and garlic. After letting it sit for fifteen minutes or so, he had coated the pork in potato starch and then deep-fried the pieces in the pan.

'The pork has been well cooked on a medium heat,' Kai told Keita.

Kotoko had already sampled it. Whenever there was a request for a remembrance meal, Kai would practise making the dish for himself first. When Kotoko had arrived for work that morning, Kai had just finished cooking, and he asked her if she would mind trying the dish.

'All right,' she had said, and taken a tentative bite, expecting it to be not quite as good as the chicken version she was used to. But she was wrong.

The piece of kara-age gave a crisp crunch as she bit into it. The texture was wonderful, the smell mouth-watering; the sesame oil, ginger and garlic tempered the richness of the meat, enhancing its flavour.

'I've never had it with pork before. It's delicious!'

'I hadn't made it before, either,' Kai said. 'Mr Miyata said pork belly kara-age was something his mother loved to cook. She was making it on the day she passed away.'

Kotoko pictured the scene. The elderly mother, cooking for her son right up until the day she died.

Once he had set out the pork kara-age on the table, Kai said gently: 'Could you please confirm every-thing looks acceptable with your remembrance meal?'

'It's fine . . .' Keita said absently, but he made no move to eat. He didn't even pick up his chopsticks, just stared intently at the two dishes in front of him.

What's wrong? wondered Kotoko. At this rate, the remembrance meal would go cold before he'd even taken a bite, and he would miss out on the miracle.

Kotoko wondered whether she should say some-thing, but Kai remained silent. And then finally Keita stirred.

'Itadakimasu,' he said, but he still didn't reach for his chopsticks. Instead, he opened his bag and took out a lunchbox.

Kotoko couldn't understand Keita's strange behaviour. Was he planning to take the pork kara-age home instead?

Keita placed the lunchbox on the table and opened the lid.

Kotoko stared at the contents. 'What—?' she couldn't help exclaiming, as her curiosity gave way to surprise. The lunchbox was crammed with . . . more pork kara-age.

I've messed things up again.

Hearing the young woman's exclamation, Keita realised his mistake. He'd done it without thinking – but of course, most people would consider it rude bringing your own packed lunch to a restaurant. He should have at least asked if it was all right first.

'I'm sorry,' he said, hastily.

'No, not at all,' Kai replied. 'Would you like me to heat that up for you? If you don't mind me doing it in the microwave.' His voice was calm and gentle, without a hint of rebuke.

Keita hesitated for a moment and then decided to take Kai up on his offer. 'Yes, please.'

'I'll leave it in the box rather than putting it out on a plate – is that all right?'

Maybe the young man was a mind-reader; it was as though he knew exactly what Keita wanted.

Kai took the lunchbox off to the kitchen. When he returned, he set it down alongside the meal he himself had cooked. Alongside the abundance of fried pork there was fluffy rice and miso soup too, and it all looked delicious.

'Please enjoy,' said Kai.

Keita had got up early that morning, and he was hungry. 'Thank you. Well . . . itadakimasu,' he said once more, putting his palms together.

First, he picked up a piece of Kai's kara-age, and bit into it with a crunch. It was pleasantly warm, though no longer piping hot. He could smell the ginger and garlic, and the delicious flavour of the meat in its soy-sauce marinade danced across his tongue. The meal may have been cooked by someone else, but it tasted exactly right – just like his mother's pork kara-age.

This dish had always been Keita's favourite. Whenever something bad happened at school his mother would make it for him, and somehow eating it had always given him the will to keep going, to struggle on with his studies and sports, though he hadn't had much of an aptitude for either.

But when it had come to the world of work, even pork kara-age hadn't been enough.

He was so ashamed – of quitting that job and shutting himself away, and above all, of the way he'd treated his mother. How could he look her in the eye? He should have taken care of her in her old age like a good son, working hard like everyone else.

When he thought of how he had failed her, and how she must have felt, it was as though a weight was pressing on his chest.

Keita had only eaten one piece of kara-age, but his appetite suddenly vanished. His arm froze, his hand still clutching his chopsticks, and his head drooped forwards with the shame. And then he heard a voice: *Don't worry. Everyone makes mistakes. Things will turn out all right in the end.*

The words came to Keita as clear as day, and gave him the strength to look up again. Maybe things really *would* be all right.

Just then the little cat mewed. '*Miaow.*'

Strange. For some reason, the cat sounded muffled.

'What's wrong?' Keita asked the kitten, and then he frowned, noticing his own voice sounded odd too.

Maybe it wasn't his voice but his hearing. He wasn't old enough to be going deaf, but perhaps the cause lay elsewhere. Keita began to feel anxious. He looked about for the restaurant staff and saw that something very strange was occurring.

Kai and the young woman had vanished, while the pendulum of the old clock had stopped swinging. And it was silent: he couldn't hear the sea or the gulls outside.

'What's going on?' he whispered, looking out of the window. And then he put his hand to his forehead. 'You're joking . . .'

The waves were motionless. They hadn't just died down: they had *stopped*. It was like looking at a photograph.

The sight came as such a shock to Keita that shadows began to crowd the edges of his vision – but this was no time to be passing out. Whatever was happening, he thought, it must be happening everywhere.

He looked over at his mobile, thinking to call someone. The charging light was glowing, so there must be power still. As he got up to reach for it, the kitten gave another short '*Miaow.*'

It was a purposeful sort of mew, as though the cat were trying to tell him something. It had turned to face the door, its little ears twitching.

'Is someone there?' Keita asked the cat. And from outside came the sound of footsteps. 'Another customer . . .?'

'*Miaow,*' the kitten mewed as if in reply, and then the door opened and Keita was struck dumb as a figure stepped into the Chibineko Kitchen.

Although it was clearly a person, Keita couldn't make out its face: there was only a blank oval, as though someone had painted it out. But even as the strange creature began to approach, Keita didn't feel frightened. He already had an inkling of who it was.

The figure walked up to Keita's table and sat down opposite him without a word, at the place-setting laid with the second portion of food.

'You can eat, if you like . . .' Keita invited timidly, and the figure gave a slight nod.

As though on cue, a cloud of steam wafted up from the pork kara-age, and the figure leaned forwards to breathe it in. And then the round-cheeked face of a woman in her sixties appeared – the face Keita had been hoping to see.

The things he had read online about the Chibineko Kitchen were true.

'Mum . . . it's you.'

Hallucination

The perception of something that is not
there. For example, seeing an object that is
not actually present, or hearing a sound
where there is none.

That was what it had said in the Kojien Japanese
dictionary.

The idea that the dead could appear was nothing
new to Keita. The elderly clients at the rehabilitation
centre were always recounting this kind of experience:
*I went out for a walk with my dead wife . . . My parents were
worried, so they came back from the other world to check up on
me . . . My friend who died in an accident showed up for a chat
about the old days . . . He's waiting for me in the next world,
that's what he told me . . . I had a visit from an old pal from
the centre . . .*

Keita had heard other stories, too: the appearance
of a childhood home that had been demolished long
ago; or the elderly person who had seen the sea in a
place where the land had long since been reclaimed.

Was Keita's mother, here in the Chibineko Kitchen,
a hallucination too? As Keita wondered, his mother
spoke.

'You've come to see me. Thank you.' Her voice was choked with emotion. It had only been a year since her death, but it was twenty years since she and Keita had looked one another in the eye and had a conversation that wasn't conducted through a door.

Keita could still picture the face of his mother in death as she lay there on the floor. He remembered how useless he had been, how incapable of helping her, and his chest grew tight again.

No words came to him. Keita had never been talkative, and the same was true of his mother. So they just sat there in silence, facing each other over the remembrance meal. The time passed quietly. Even the little kitten didn't open its mouth to mew. Then from out of that peaceful stillness, words came to Keita's mind.

The dead can only stay for as long as the remembrance meal is still steaming.

That was what the restaurant owner's blog had said, and Keita realised the time he had with his mother was finite. *I have to say something*, he thought, but still the words wouldn't come.

He'd ordered a remembrance meal, he'd made it this far, but now the minutes were slipping away.

Once again, he was proving utterly useless.

Keita clenched his jaw in frustration, just as a buzzing started up from over by the old clock. His mobile was flashing with a message.

He went over to pick it up, and there, displayed on the screen, was the name *Shiori*. It was a message from his manager at the rehabilitation centre. The woman who was always pushing Keita around and telling him off.

All it said was: 'You can do it.'

A year before, Keita had been very close to quitting his job at the rehabilitation centre. In the end, however, he had decided to stick it out, dreading the thought of going to any other interviews; he was sure he'd only be laughed at and rejected.

Though he hated that he kept making mistakes at the centre, at least he was earning enough money to live on. What was more, a lot of the staff and clients at the centre remembered his mother and, bit by bit, people were beginning to speak to him. But they didn't refer to him by his surname, as would have been usual for a staff member, instead calling him 'Keita-kun', as though he were just a boy. It made him feel embarrassed but happy: conversation had been lacking in his life.

Even those who hadn't known his mother would talk to him. One such person was Takao Kaburaki.

'I'm sorry I landed you in trouble back then, son,' he said to Keita during one shift.

It was Kaburaki's hand Keita had taken that day; Shiori had given him a talking-to for attempting to lead the old man to the bathroom.

'No, it's my fault. I wasn't thinking,' Keita said. He really meant it, and not just because of Shiori's scolding. He had come to learn more about Kaburaki: the old man wanted to get to the stage where he could manage by himself, so that he could return home. But not for his own sake.

'It's my wife – she'll be lonely, you see?' Kaburaki had said.

His wife had in fact already passed away, but Kaburaki's remark wasn't intended as a joke, and nor was it brought on by dementia. 'My wife always loved that house. And I just know that she's still there, waiting for me to come home.'

Kaburaki had no children. After his wife passed away and he went into hospital, he told Keita, the house was left as good as empty.

'So I've got to get back there quickly. Or she'll give me an earful. I made her a promise when we got married, after all.'

'A promise?'

'Yes. Told her I'd always look after her, didn't I? That I'd never leave her lonely. A right job it's turned out to be, I don't mind telling you!' he finished, but the warmth in his eyes belied his words.

Shiori knew about this too, apparently: Kaburaki had told Keita that, every so often, she would go and look in on his empty house for him.

'She's sharp-tongued, but she has a good heart, taking care of an old man like me. Don't think badly of her,' he said. He seemed to want to smooth things over between them. Shiori was clearly well-liked, not just by Kaburaki but by the other residents too. 'I know she can be harsh, but she means well. So don't let it get to you, son.'

'All right . . . I won't,' Keita replied, regretting now the way he had reacted to Shiori's stern words that day.

Early one morning, a cold drizzle began to fall. Keita knew it would be a busy shift; the clients always complained of aches and pains and low moods in bad weather. He resolved to work hard and not get under the feet of the other staff.

As he reached the centre, he noticed a cardboard box had been left outside the main entrance. Before he had time to wonder what was inside, he heard a feeble '*Miaow* . . .'

'Wait, is that . . .?' He peered into the box and there, sure enough, was a kitten. It was tiny, with black-and-white splotchy markings like a cow, and black patches over its eyes as though it was wearing a mask.

An abandoned cat. It didn't happen so much nowadays, but there must still be people out there who would disown a newborn kitten.

'How awful!

The little thing was shivering; Keita was sure it would die if left to fend for itself on a rainy day like this one. He couldn't bear to see it so miserable, and he held out his umbrella to shelter it.

'*Miaow*,' the kitten mewed, as though in thanks, but Keita was too busy fretting to reply. What should he do? He couldn't just leave it there, but he could hardly take it into work, either. He knew that some of the clients at the rehabilitation centre were allergic.

He thought about taking the day off, but where would he go with the little cat? His landlord didn't allow pets, and he'd spent so much of his life shut away that he didn't have any friends – or even any acquaintances – he could ask to take care of it.

Keita stood there helplessly, still holding his umbrella over the cardboard box, letting the cold rain fall on his back.

'*Miaow?*'

The kitten was looking up at Keita, its sweet little face puzzled. He racked his brains for a way to rescue it, but got nowhere, the rain steadily soaking into his clothes. And then a voice cut through the air.

'What are you doing?'

Shiori. She was probably on her way home; she wore the fatigued look of someone just getting off the night shift.

Shiori was a stickler for punctuality, and Keita was sure she was going to tell him off for dawdling by the doors. But he was wrong.

'Oh, a cat!' she said, crouching down by the cardboard box.

'I think someone must have dumped it here,' Keita said, standing to attention as though he had started his shift already. Shiori made him nervous.

'I can see that,' she said drily, yet there was a tender look in her eye. Crouching down on the ground, Keita's fierce boss looked somehow childlike.

'What are you going to do with it?' Shiori asked, still peering into the box.

'Well, I . . .' Keita didn't know what to say.

Shiori seemed to understand, without him explaining any further. 'Hmph. I see,' she muttered. And then she gave Keita an order: 'Go and start your shift.'

'But . . .' Was she was telling him to abandon the cat?

But no – Shiori's next words came as a surprise. 'It's all right,' she said. 'I'll take it to the vet, and then it can come home with me.'

'Really?'

'Yes. It can be my guard cat. It's a dangerous world we live in, after all.'

'A guard cat?' Keita echoed. What use would a newborn kitten be?

'It's fine, you just get to work,' said Shiori. 'Leave the cat to me, and you go and look after our clients.' She picked up the kitten and held it against her chest, apparently unconcerned that she might get her clothes dirty. The kitten trembled a little at first, as though in alarm, but then clung on tight.

Evening fell, and Keita's shift came to an end. He was just leaving the rehabilitation centre when his phone rang.

He assumed it must be one of his colleagues. No one else had his number, and the centre was so understaffed it wasn't uncommon to be called back in to cover someone's shift. Keita had nothing to do at home, so he always answered these calls, even on his days off.

He looked at the screen now, and saw the name displayed there: *Shiori – work.*

'Hello?' Keita answered.

'I'm sorry to call you – it's nothing to do with work,' Shiori began.

Nothing to do with work? If she wasn't phoning to ask Keita to do overtime, then what could she want?

'The cat's fine,' Shiori continued abruptly.

'What?'

'The kitten. From this morning. I took him to the vet, and they said he's all right.'

Keita heard the kitten give a well-timed '*Miaow,*' as though attesting to Shiori's words. The sound came through clearly over the phone and Keita pictured her cradling the black-masked kitten in her arms as she talked.

'I just thought you might be worried,' Shiori said, as though to justify the call. But Keita had known the kitten would be safe and happy in Shiori's care. 'That was all,' she finished, and hung up without giving Keita time to reply.

*

A few days later, Keita found himself finishing work at the same time as Shiori. He waited until they were alone, and then held out an envelope. 'Here, boss.'

'What's this?'

'For the vet bill,' Keita said. He had looked online to find out roughly how much the appointment would have cost and had brought in the money for her.

But Shiori shook her head. 'It's fine. He's my cat now, anyway.'

'But it was me who found him,' Keita said. As Shiori had given the abandoned kitten a home, he felt it was the least he could do.

Shiori considered this for a moment. 'All right,' she said finally, and took the envelope.

It contained almost all of Keita's savings. He'd have to make some cutbacks, but he was pleased and relieved that she had accepted the money.

'Well, see you tomorrow,' he said. He was about to turn and head home when Shiori stopped him.

'Wait a minute.'

'Um—?'

'Do you want to come over and see the cat? If you've got time.'

'What?'

'Now that you've paid for its bills it's your cat too, Keita-kun.' Shiori had tagged on 'kun' like always, as though Keita were the younger one – only this time her words had come out in a rush. 'If you'd rather not, it's fine,' she said.

'No, I'd like to, but . . . are you sure I won't be a bother?' Keita said, wondering briefly whether Shiori had a family. But she told him that her parents had passed away, and she didn't have any siblings.

'It's fine, I live alone,' she said.

'Hachisuke, we've got a visitor,' Shiori called out as she opened the front door. She had told Keita on the way home that she'd chosen the name Hachisuke because of the kitten's black-mask pattern: his face was split into black and white like the character for eight, or 'hachi': 八

It looked as though Hachisuke had been waiting for Shiori to return home. He was sitting just inside the hallway and he mewed in reply, then came and nuzzled up against Keita's legs as though he remembered him.

Keita stroked Hachisuke's head, and the cat gave a rumbling purr.

'I think someone likes you, Keita!' Shiori said.

Keita's heart thudded. He knew she was just joking, pretending to speak for the kitten, but still his pulse began racing.

With a sudden thrill of surprise, Keita realised what was happening.

He was falling for his boss.

Why have I developed these feelings? he asked himself, his mind going round and round in circles. *And what am I supposed to do about them?*

No, there was no need to do anything. A middle-aged man who'd shut himself away for two decades had no right to fall in love with anyone. He would be a bachelor his whole life. But, thanks to the kitten, he'd been able to spend some time alone with Shiori. He would be content with that.

Shiori's voice broke into his thoughts. 'We just got off work, you must be hungry. I don't have much in the house, but I'll make us something.'

'You don't have to . . .'

'Look, I need to eat anyway, so you might as well stay. Don't expect anything fancy, though.'

Shiori showed Keita into the house, and then she cooked him a meal. Keita could hardly breathe – but it was wonderful.

*

A week passed and Keita went to work as usual, keeping his feelings for Shiori hidden.

Then one day, Shiori didn't come in. She had phoned the centre first thing to say that she had a fever.

Keita had never known Shiori to come down with a cold, but the staff member who had spoken to her assured him that it wasn't serious. 'She said she's staying at home to be on the safe side.' Everyone seemed to think she was just trying to avoid infecting the centre's elderly residents. Some of the staff actually joked about it: 'Even the devil runs a temperature sometimes!'

But Keita was worried. Shiori might suddenly get worse. And even if she didn't, it was miserable being ill when you lived alone. Did she have food? Medicine? Had she been to the hospital? What if she had collapsed?

Keita thought of his mother, lying on the floor by the sink. He had learned back then that no one is invulnerable, no matter how robust they seem.

He decided to go to Shiori's house as soon as his shift was over.

Keita bought some fruit and cold medicine on the way. He didn't plan on going inside, just handing over the things he'd brought Shiori and going home.

He had no trouble remembering the way, and soon he was outside Shiori's door. But Keita found he didn't have the courage to ring the bell. He stepped back for a moment, rocking from foot to foot on the doorstep and trying to work up the nerve, but it was no good.

'I'll only be disturbing her,' he muttered finally. He should have called first. In fact, he should never have come at all. He thought about leaving the medicine and fruit at the door, but Shiori would probably be creeped out. She might even report him for it. And she was the one person whose good opinion mattered to Keita.

He decided to just go home. It would be as if nothing had ever happened.

Keita was just turning to leave when from down at his feet he heard a familiar '*miaow*'.

He glanced down and there was Hachisuke sitting on the street, looking up at him with an air of bemusement.

'What are you doing out here?' Keita said.

'*Miaow.*'

'No, not *miaow*—'

'*Miaow.*'

As Keita stood there, mid-conversation with the kitten, he heard the door open behind him. This was followed by a yell: 'Keita-kun? Grab Hachisuke!'

Shiori was standing in the doorway, clad in her pyjamas.

The mystery of how Hachisuke had escaped out onto the street was soon solved. Shiori had opened a window to let in some fresh air, and the kitten had slipped through the gap.

'Thank goodness you were there, Keita-kun. Seriously, thank you,' Shiori said. Her voice was as firm and assured as always, and her face looked a healthy colour, too. She must be on the mend.

The next moment, Keita realised she was inviting him inside. 'Come on, at least have some tea,' she said, and he hesitantly accepted.

'These are for you, boss,' he said, handing over the medicine and fruit. Shiori smiled. Keita noticed she seemed much more relaxed at home than at work.

'Thank you, Keita-kun, that's really nice of you. I bet you're popular with the ladies.'

'Please, don't make fun of me.'

'I'm not! You're kind to women, you're kind to cats – you're a catch.'

'I don't think I've ever been considered a catch in my life,' Keita said, and meant it. Girls had never paid him any attention in his school years, and he'd locked himself away not long after that. Looking back now, he couldn't recall talking to any women other than his mother.

He told Shiori this truthfully, and she frowned slightly.

'Really? Well, you know, I don't dislike you, Keita-kun.'

His heart pounded. He knew she was only teasing him, but he couldn't let her words pass without remark.

'Do you mean it?' he said. 'You really don't hate me?'

It wasn't the sort of thing for a man pushing forty to ask, but love brings out the childish side of people. He was under no illusions that Shiori would give him the answer he wanted to hear, and the moment he spoke, he regretted it. She was sure to laugh at him. Either that or shy away in disgust.

But Shiori did neither. Instead she said, her expression earnest, 'If I didn't like you, I wouldn't have let you into my house.'

This was enough for Keita. He opened his mouth to say a delighted *Thank you*, but those weren't the words that came tumbling out.

'I really like you.'

Keita hadn't intended to confess his love to Shiori, and he surprised himself even more than her. But he simply hadn't been able to contain his feelings.

Shiori said nothing. She sat there looking at Keita, Hachisuke on her lap. Keita had no idea what she was thinking, but there was no turning back now.

'I've been hiding away in my room for twenty years, and I'll be forty soon,' he continued. 'I don't have any savings, and I only have a part-time job . . . but I like you. I really like you, boss. I'm sorry . . .'

Both his voice and his body shook. There was silence – but not for long.

'Ugh, really?' Shiori said.

Her words were like a slap in the face, and Keita's heart sank. So that was how she really felt. He had known all along that his feelings would be nothing more than an annoyance to her. And now things would be awkward at work, too.

But Shiori wasn't finished.

'Don't put yourself down like that when you're trying to talk a woman round. Don't *apologise*. So, you like me – tell me what you want to do about it!'

'What?' Keita's eyes widened in shock.

'Tell me again, properly this time,' Shiori continued, unsmiling. 'And don't call me boss – use my name.'

'Um . . . okay, b–boss. Well, I—'

'Not boss! *Shiori*. My name is Shiori.'

Keita's heart was thumping so hard now he felt she

must hear it, but somehow he managed to force the words out. 'I . . . I love you, Shiori,' he said.

He had done it – he had told her how he felt.

And when the reply came, he could hardly believe his ears.

'I feel the same,' said Shiori.

Keita's heart nearly stopped altogether. He couldn't take it in. As he sat there, mouth gaping, she continued: 'Me and Hachisuke love you too, Keita-kun.'

The little cat was looking at him intently. Keita felt a prickling sensation behind his nose, and as tears spilled from his eyes, it was all he could do to say, 'Thank you so much.'

He knew he was being pathetic, even at a moment like this. But he was happy, because Shiori loved him.

In his phone's contact list, she went from being *Shiori – work* to just *Shiori*, and then, six months later, they were married and she became Shiori Miyata.

Keita passed his care worker basic training and began working full time at the rehabilitation centre. His life was changing so fast he could barely keep up.

Twenty years as a recluse had left him with huge challenges to overcome, and he was quick to lose heart. But every time, Shiori picked him back up.

'Don't worry – remember, me and Hachisuke love you. Don't let it get you down. Everyone makes mistakes. Things will turn out all right in the end.'

And Keita believed her. Shiori had cast some kind of spell on him, one that made him want to put everything into living. His life wasn't over yet.

But there was one more person who had given Keita strength. And so he had come to this restaurant, where miracles happened, to tell his mother the news.

'Mum, thank you for being here. I know I wasn't a good son to you – but I'm glad I was born. I'm finally happy, so happy.'

Keita and his mother sat opposite each other by the window of the Chibineko Kitchen. He had never thought the day would come when he would say that, and mean it. But, somehow, wanting to make Shiori happy had brought him happiness of his own. He only wished that he had thought to make his mother happy when he had the chance.

His nose was stinging but there was no time for crying. He had spent too long telling his mother his story, and the steam rising up from the pork kara-age was beginning to fade away. Their parting was drawing near.

His mother sensed it too. 'So you came here to let me know that you're married,' she said. Even now, in death, her thoughts were with Keita.

But Keita shook his head. 'No. That's not all.'

'It's not?'

'There's one more thing I wanted to tell you, Mum.'

If he went home without saying it, he'd get a ticking off from his wife.

Keita gestured towards the lunchbox filled with pork kara-age. 'It was Shiori who cooked this.'

'Was it? Goodness me . . .' his mother said, fondly. She knew Keita's wife. After all, it was she who had trained Shiori as a carer, fifteen years before.

'You know, Keita-kun, I actually heard all about you before we met, from my supervisor, Ms Miyata – your mum, I mean,' Shiori had told him, in the days after they had starting seeing each other.

Keita had never known that his mother had been a manager at the centre, just as Shiori was now. And there were other revelations.

'I was like you, Keita-kun. I was no good at smiling, either,' Shiori continued. She had found it hard to talk to people too, she said, and had often longed to quit. But she hadn't always been that way.

'When I was in my third year at primary school, I watched my parents die right in front of me. We were walking home from a restaurant, just talking about something or other, laughing, and then suddenly this man came out of nowhere and attacked us. My mum and dad put themselves in his way to protect me, and they were both stabbed. I couldn't smile after that.' Shiori's voice was dark. The wound was raw, even now.

Shiori had known that it was important to smile – it cheered up the residents at the rehabilitation centre – and she had felt that if she couldn't manage it then she shouldn't be there. She would only be a nuisance to the other staff. And so she tried to quit.

But Keita's mother had sat her down and listened to her story. 'Don't worry,' she told Shiori when she had finished. 'You're such a kind person, and the others will understand. It's all right. Everything will be all right.' And then she had told Shiori all about her son. About how, even though he had shut himself away, she knew he would be fine.

'She talked about how kind you were, Keita-kun, and how you always tried your best to make things easier for her.'

So his mother had believed in him, despite everything. Keita's eyes welled up, as he realised just how much she had done for him.

Keita had been taught the ropes at work by Shiori and so, in a roundabout way, those lessons had come down to him from his mother.

And his mother's legacy would continue in other ways, too.

'How old should a child be before they first try pork kara-age?' Keita asked his mother, tears springing to his eyes again. He set his mouth in a firm line but he couldn't hold them back, and his mother's face blurred before him.

'How old? Are you saying—?'

It sounded as though she had caught on.

'That's right,' Keita said. 'We're having a baby. You're going to be a grandma, Mum.'

That was what he had gone there to tell her. He was having a child with Shiori, the person he loved most in the world.

But Shiori's news had brought with it new concerns. Their finances, for one thing. Keita continued scrimping and saving every yen of his wage – which was higher now that he was working full-time. He didn't need anything for himself; he wanted to spend every-thing on his family.

And the fact that he would be sixty by the time their child was grown worried him too. But what really kept Keita up at night was the thought that their child might end up becoming a recluse, just as he had.

'It's all right,' Shiori had reassured him when he shared his fears with her.

'You mean you don't think it'll happen?'

'No, I don't mean that. I mean, I think that everyone trips up sometimes. Everyone has moments when they just want to run away.'

Keita knew it was true. Life was difficult, painful. Even now, when he'd found happiness, there were still days when he didn't want to leave the house.

'But it's okay,' Shiori continued to Keita, and to the baby inside her. 'If our child shuts themself away I'll do what your mother did, Keita-kun. I'll trust in them, I'll believe they'll be happy some day and that it will be all right, come what may – and I'll make them pork kara-age. I'll keep on making it, as many times as I have to.'

A parent's cooking is a powerful thing – imbued as it is with love and with hopes for their child's happiness.

*

Keita thanked his mother again.

'So you really did find happiness,' she whispered, tearfully.

'Yes. Thanks to Shiori, and to our baby that's on the way – and thanks to you, Mum. I'm the happiest person in the world.' He said the words with certainty.

'You're such a good son, Keita.'

'A good son?' Keita was suddenly incredulous. 'You can't be serious.'

It just wasn't true, no matter which way he looked at it. Keita thought of all the times he had failed to even reply when his mother spoke to him through the door.

But she didn't retract her words. 'You know, what brings a parent the most joy is seeing their child happy. I'm sure you'll come to understand that too,' she continued softly.

But Keita already understood perfectly. Nothing would delight him more than if the child who was soon to enter his life could find happiness.

'Now I don't have anything left to worry about,' said his mother. 'Thanks to you, Keita. I'm so grateful. I'm so glad you were my child. Thank you, thank you . . .' His mother was still saying it as she faded away.

Keita heard her footsteps receding and, moments later, the door to the Chibineko Kitchen opened and closed.

The pork kara-age had gone completely cold. There was no more steam. Keita placed his palms together before the remembrance meal.

Thank you, Mum, he mouthed soundlessly, over and over like a prayer.

Only Keita experienced the miracle – to Kotoko and Kai, it appeared as though he was just sitting alone at the table.

They didn't speak to their diners while the remembrance meal was still warm; today, too, they had simply stood quietly in the corner of the room. Chibi was asleep on the rocking chair. Kotoko liked these peaceful moments at the restaurant.

The hushed silence seemed as if it would go on for ever. But then the steam faded, and Keita, hands joined as though in prayer before the now-cold remembrance meal, began to speak under his breath: *Thank you, Mum*.

Kotoko heard him mouthing the words again and again, tears in his eyes. He must have seen his mother, then.

Kai had evidently noticed this too, and he went off to brew some tea, which he brought over to the table.

'Here you are,' he said, and Keita glanced up, startled.

'Thank you. For giving me this miracle,' he said.

Keita told Kai and Kotoko what he and his mother had talked about. They learned about Keita's marriage, his cat Hachisuke, his job at the rehabilitation centre.

'I'm very sorry I was so late,' Keita apologised again. He explained how he had been on the bus when he had noticed an elderly passenger acting strangely. 'I think she had dementia,' he said. Recognising the signs from his work at the centre, he hadn't felt he could leave her wandering about on her own – she might be targeted by purse snatchers, or stumble out into traffic.

So Keita had jumped off the bus. He had stopped the old lady and spoken to her, before taking her to the local police station. He would have called the restaurant, he said, but he had drained his phone battery looking at the map, and there were no payphones nearby. So instead he had returned to the bus stop and caught the next bus to the restaurant.

'I'm really sorry,' he said again.

He had done an admirable thing, Kotoko thought, and yet he was shrinking into himself as though he had done something wrong. He seemed such a gentle man; she could understand why Shiori had married him.

'Could I come back again sometime?' Keita asked. 'I would love to bring my wife and our child.'

He was obviously taken with the Chibineko Kitchen. Kai's cooking warmed the soul and captured people's hearts; it had captured Kotoko's, too.

Before Kai could reply, Chibi, having woken up, responded with a short mew of protest. Both Keita and Kotoko grasped his meaning straight away.

'And may I bring Hachisuke?' he asked. It was the little black-and-white cat who had brought Keita and Shiori together, after all. He was an important member of the family.

What could Kai say but yes?

'Of course. You're very welcome to visit us again – we'll be waiting with something delicious for you,' he said, and Chibi gave a satisfied '*Miaow*'.

A special recipe from the
Chibineko Kitchen

Buta Bara no Kara-age: Fried pork belly

Ingredients (serves 2)
- 200g pork belly, thinly sliced
- 2 tsp cooking saké
- 1 tsp soy sauce
- Salt, black pepper – to taste
- Grated ginger, grated garlic – to taste
- Potato starch (katakuriko) or flour – enough to coat the pork with
- Sesame oil for frying

Method
1. Cut the sliced pork into bite-sized pieces.
2. Combine the saké, soy sauce, salt, black pepper, ginger and garlic and spoon the mixture into a freezer bag. Add the pieces of pork to the bag

and massage well to coat the pork in the mixture.

3. Heat the sesame oil in a frying pan. Coat the pieces of seasoned pork with potato starch or flour and fry them slowly on medium heat.

Tips

As the pork is thinly sliced, you should be able to shallow fry it using a relatively small amount of oil. (But it will also turn out delicious if deep-fried!)

3

A cat called Sora, and soy-glazed sardines on rice

イワシ
Sardines

Sardine fishing off Chiba Prefecture's Kujukuri Beach dates back to the Edo period and it remains a thriving industry today. Local restaurants all feature sardines on their menus, and products like pickled Kujukuri sardines with sesame, from marine food company Kaneyon Suisan, are also popular.

'You're being taken for a ride,' Fujii said, with finality.

Mitsuyo Yamada was sitting in the rehabilitation centre, sipping her tea. She wasn't a resident there, but once or twice a week the centre ran coffee mornings for over sixty-fives.

She would be seventy this year, but Mitsuyo didn't particularly care for being treated like an old person. She did like the place, though. The building was clean and airy and the staff were polite and friendly. Anyway, she had nowhere else to go and it cost very little to come here for a cup of tea and a chat.

Some of the other senior citizens, however, could be terribly officious.

'It'll be some kind of bank-transfer scam, you mark my words. You should steer well clear of it. Could even be one of those dodgy religious organisations,' Fujii continued to lecture. He was hard of hearing, and his voice was awfully loud.

The coffee morning was for older people who were in good health and living independently; the centre was really just providing a space where they could come and socialise. A member of staff would poke their head around the door from time to time, but mostly they just left the senior citizens to their own devices.

'It's not a con, and it's not some questionable religious group either. They're not out to get me – I was the one who got in contact with *them*,' Mitsuyo replied, mildly. She didn't like quarrelling, but she could hardly just stay silent.

'You shouldn't go,' Fujii said doggedly. At seventy-three, he was three years older than Mitsuyo. Both of them lived alone and neither had much contact with their families. They exchanged New Year's cards, but they never saw each other outside the rehabilitation centre – or the hospital waiting room. Still, Fujii was one of the few people Mitsuyo spoke to. She didn't work, and her days were spent between her home, the centre and the hospital.

Mitsuyo had been born into an era when things were good, and now she received a modest pension on which she could just about get by. She had the house and the savings her husband had left her, too. But even if it cost her all those savings, even if she had to use up her precious pension, there was someone Mitsuyo wanted to see.

And she had made the mistake of telling Fujii about this when she had bumped into him at the hospital the other day.

'Of course it's a con!' chimed in Tomomi Hirakawa, putting down her tea. 'You can't meet someone who's dead! You look gullible, Mitsuyo. They'll browbeat you into buying an expensive inkan stamp or a vase or something – this kind of thing happens *all* the time.'

Tomomi was the same age as Mitsuyo – if she was to be believed – but she wasn't Mitsuyo's cup of tea. Tomomi tended to pass judgement without listening to the other side of the story, and whenever they spoke Mitsuyo couldn't help but get the impression Tomomi thought she was a fool.

Fujii and Tomomi weren't the only ones opposed to Mitsuyo's plan.

'I don't think you should go either.' A low voice entered the discussion: Kanayama. He had been a carpenter back in his working days. Mitsuyo guessed he must be pushing eighty. He was a quiet man, and even when they ran into each other in the hospital, they exchanged few words.

Old-fashioned, serious chap that he was, he seemed genuinely worried for her. Mitsuyo remembered seeing him at her husband's funeral, a gift of incense in his hand. But while Mitsuyo liked Kanayama, she didn't appreciate his worrying about her.

In fact, she realised, she was on the verge of telling the lot of them that she didn't care if it *was* a scam, she simply wished they would all just leave the matter alone.

'There's this restaurant where they say you can meet someone who's dead.'

So Mitsuyo had been told by an old man called Kaburaki. And he hadn't been talking about hiring a medium or anything like that – he had said the dead person was supposed to appear right in front of you.

Kaburaki used to be a resident at the centre, and had come along to the coffee mornings from time to time. Used to, because now his illness had come back and he'd been admitted to a hospital some way away. Mitsuyo had been to see him, and that was when he had told her about the restaurant.

Kaburaki had had a stroke, on top of everything else, and he had explained to Mitsuyo he would probably never be well enough to leave hospital now. 'I wanted to get back to my house while I was still alive, to see my wife. But my body's just not up to it.'

Mitsuyo didn't know the exact details of his condition, but she could guess. He was, after all, on the palliative care ward.

'I'll come and visit you again,' she had said on her way out, but Kaburaki had waved her away.

'No, that's all right. Life's too short. You spend your time doing the things you want to do,' he replied. Then he had handed her a piece of paper on which was written the name and phone number of the Chibineko Kitchen.

*

121

A place where the dead could come back to you . . . it was absurd. It probably *was* a scam, like Fujii and the others said. Maybe Mitsuyo was about to be swindled out of her money, or become mixed up with dangerous people. Perhaps she wouldn't even make it out alive.

Mitsuyo was prepared for anything.

Fine, she told Fujii and the others in her head. *If I end up getting conned, that's fine. What's the point in an old person like me clinging on to money anyway? Besides, I've lived long enough.*

She left them to their coffee morning, saying she had things to get on with. She had nothing of the sort, of course; she just wanted to be alone.

The next day, Mitsuyo set out for the Chibineko Kitchen. She had decided to take the first train of the morning.

She hadn't been on a train since going to visit Kaburaki in hospital. She could remember her last journey before that one, too; it had been two years ago, when she had travelled to Shinjuku to see a Ken'ichi Kawakubo concert.

Mitsuyo was as loyal to Ken'ichi Kawakubo as young fans were to their favourite pop idols. He might not be a household name, but she had been going to his concerts since she was in high school, and for as long as she was still mobile she intended to carry on.

Mitsuyo had often listened to his music with her cat, a Russian blue with gorgeous fur – named Sora, like the sky. Her husband had brought Sora home about six months before he died. He wasn't an animal lover himself, and Mitsuyo couldn't understand at first what had made him decide to part with a not-insignificant sum of money for the creature. But then, one day, while she was outside weeding the garden, she overheard her husband speaking inside the house.

'You look after my wife, all right? She gets lonely,' her husband was telling the cat, unaware that Mitsuyo could hear him.

Mitsuyo's husband was several years older than she was, and he hadn't been well. He was going into the hospital the following week for some tests.

'I'm counting on you,' he had continued to Sora, his tone serious.

Mitsuyo had realised he was worrying about what would happen to her after he died. *A cat can't possibly look after a person!* But, as ridiculous as it had sounded, Mitsuyo hadn't felt like laughing. Instead, her eyes prickled. Afraid that she might sob out loud, she had

123

moved further into the garden so her husband wouldn't hear her.

The test results weren't good; it turned out to be cancer. Her husband also suffered from diabetes, which had damaged his blood vessels and meant he couldn't undergo surgery. His condition had slowly deteriorated until he passed away, three years ago now.

After he died, Mitsuyo and Sora had only each other. And the cat never seemed to want to leave Mitsuyo's side. 'You're taking good care of me, aren't you?' Mitsuyo would whisper, her eyes filling with tears. Then, determined not to spend all her time crying, she would put on some music to listen to with Sora.

'This is a beautiful tune, isn't it? I love when Ken'ichi sings the Beatles.'

Ken'ichi Kawakubo did write and perform his own music, but he often sang Beatles songs at his concerts too. Mitsuyo's life had been lived in anticipation of the next concert: she was lonely, but Sora and Ken'ichi Kawakubo helped her to keep going.

And then, one year ago, even these comforts had been taken from her. Ken'ichi had passed away, and by some cruel trick of fate Sora died too, as though following Mitsuyo's favourite singer into death.

So now Mitsuyo was alone. And she had been feeling as though the loneliness might just about crush her, until Kaburaki had told her about the Chibineko Kitchen.

There's this restaurant where they say you can meet someone who's dead.

A young woman, reunited with the brother she had lost in a traffic accident. A primary-school boy who had met the very first girl he had loved. An old man professing his love to his wife in the next world. A young man who had spoken to his departed parents . . . Kaburaki had told Mitsuyo about these people. He must have heard about the place from someone else, but he spoke of it as though from first-hand experience.

The stories were hard to believe – the tall tales of a stroke-addled old man – yet Mitsuyo clung to them.

She had taken home the piece of paper Kaburaki had handed her and phoned the restaurant. A young man answered.

'This is the Chibineko Kitchen. Thank you for your call.'

The voice was polite, gentle, and Mitsuyo felt instant relief; there seemed nothing frightening about the person on the other end of the line, at least.

'I would like to order a remembrance meal,' she said, decisively.

'Certainly,' the young man replied.

So such a thing *did* exist. Of course, it might still turn out to be a scam, but as Mitsuyo had no way of checking she felt there was little point in worrying about that now.

'Could I have your name and telephone number? And please tell me the meal you would like us to prepare,' continued the man.

Mitsuyo gave him her details, he thanked her, and it seemed the call was over. Now all she had to do was find her way to the restaurant. She was about to hang up, when from the other end of the line came a '*Miaow.*'

This was followed by the young man saying hastily: 'We have a cat at the restaurant – I hope that won't be a problem for you?'

That explained the mewing. And given that 'Chibineko' meant 'little cat', it didn't come as too much of a surprise.

'That's fine,' said Mitsuyo, recalling her own late Sora.

'Excellent, thank you.'

'*Miaow.*'

The young man's words mingled with the cat's mew. It was as though the cat were thanking Mitsuyo too, and she couldn't help but chuckle.

'Could I possibly ask you to go and meet our guest off the bus?' Kai said to Kotoko.

The Chibineko Kitchen was on the outskirts of the seaside town, and customers had to make their way along the beach before they saw it. Kotoko remembered her first visit; she had wondered whether there really would be a restaurant there. A lot of visitors must feel similarly anxious – and today's guest was a lady of seventy, so it wouldn't do to let her get lost.

'Of course. I'll be back soon,' Kotoko replied, and headed for the door.

It was a mild day for December, and the place was awash in gentle sunlight. Kotoko was thinking that it almost felt like spring when she heard a noise at her feet.

'*Miaow.*'

Kotoko knew who that voice belonged to, and looked down.

Outside the door to the Chibineko Kitchen was a chalkboard, and beside it sat a white kitten with ginger patches – Chibi, the restaurant's cat. He wasn't supposed to be outside, but he had a habit of escaping.

Kotoko was sure the windows and door had been shut, and yet here he was.

'*Miaow.*' Chibi's face wore a satisfied expression. He loved it out here, under the blue sky.

Kotoko found her mouth twitching into a smile, but she quickly pursed her lips. They were well away from any busy roads here, but there were still dangers that could befall a kitten. Chibi could get lost, or be attacked by crows. There might be stray cats around, and if the little kitten got into a fight with one he could get badly hurt, or infected with some disease.

Kotoko knew Kai would be devastated if anything happened to Chibi, as would she, so she told him off with all the severity she could muster. 'You're not allowed outside! Understand?' Scolding didn't come naturally to her, however, and even she could hear she wasn't very intimidating.

'*Miaow,*' Chibi mewed briefly, as if in reply, although Kotoko doubted how much he had actually understood. So she stood there, glowering at him, until he padded back into the restaurant.

Mitsuyo was growing anxious.

She had made it to the town Kaburaki had told her about, but when she stepped off the train she couldn't see or even smell the sea. Her confidence faltered; she knew the Chibineko Kitchen was supposed to be on the coast. Had she perhaps got off at the wrong stop?

She checked the station name again, and it matched the one written on her piece of paper. This was the right place. She considered asking a station attendant just to make sure, but there was no one around. *You hardly see staff anymore, not since they started putting in those automatic ticket gates.*

She knew she might find someone in the station office who could help her, but Mitsuyo was feeling too impatient; getting older made even the smallest things seem like too much effort.

She made her way out of the station and found the bus stop. Someone from the Chibineko Kitchen was supposed to be meeting her at the other end, but even after boarding the bus she had been advised to, she felt uneasy. *I do hope I get there all right . . .*

There were no other passengers on the bus, only Mitsuyo and the driver. Looking out of the window she saw that the streets were deserted. A good number of the houses by the road appeared unoccupied, and the small factory they passed seemed to be disused.

Eventually, the bus drew up to Mitsuyo's stop and she got off.

There was a girl standing there. She had a sort of old-fashioned elegance, and looked to be around twenty. Mitsuyo thought she was going to get onto the bus, but she made no move towards the door. Instead she addressed Mitsuyo.

'Hello – I'm Kotoko Niki, from the Chibineko Kitchen. You must be Mrs Yamada?'

'Oh . . . yes.'

'I'm here to show you to the restaurant.'

Mitsuyo breathed a sigh of relief. Now she could be sure of finding the place.

The girl's polite, unassuming manner reassured Mitsuyo – Kotoko had addressed her by name, as everybody had used to. Back then, if Mitsuyo had been shopping and the store had a new assistant, the shopkeeper might say, 'She's just moved up from the country last month, Mrs Yamada. She doesn't know the ropes yet – so I hope you'll treat her kindly.' The young shop girl would bow her head shyly and say, 'Pleased to meet you,' and then every time Mitsuyo went shopping after that, she would say: 'Lovely to see you again, Mrs Yamada!' while Mitsuyo would be sure to remember the names of the young shop girls and boys, too.

But times had changed. There were no shops like that left anymore, not where Mitsuyo lived. One by one the greengrocers and fishmongers and rice shops had all closed their doors. Nowadays she shopped online, or bought her groceries at the supermarket, where it was possible to do your shopping without exchanging a word with anyone. You never knew who the shopkeeper was.

Even in the hospital they would call you by a number rather than your name.

And yet here was the girl from the Chibineko Kitchen addressing Mitsuyo properly.

Kotoko gave a little bow of her head. 'We'll have to walk the last bit. I'm very sorry, but we don't have a car,' she said.

'Oh, don't worry. I may look old, but my legs won't let me down. Besides, I like walking,' Mitsuyo replied.

Her earlier worries had vanished without a trace.

A river ran alongside the road that led to the Chibineko Kitchen. It was quiet there too; no one else was on the riverbank.

'This is the Koitogawa,' said Kotoko. Mitsuyo had never heard of it, but Kotoko said it was the third-longest river in Chiba. Sunlight sparkled on the surface of the water.

'If you carry on along this road, you come out at Tokyo Bay,' Kotoko said, pointing.

It was warm in the sun, the perfect weather for walking, and Mitsuyo felt carefree and happy as she strolled along with Kotoko.

They reached the sea in less than ten minutes. Dozens of seabirds were wheeling overhead, mewling: '*Miaoow, miaoow.*'

'They're black-tailed gulls. Sea cats,' Kotoko said.

It was Mitsuyo's first time coming across them. Those forlorn calls really did sound like the cries of a stray kitten, she thought.

Mitsuyo and Kotoko walked along the empty beach together. While it didn't seem a very lively town, the place didn't feel desolate either. If anything, the quiet was a relief for Mitsuyo.

'The restaurant is this way,' Kotoko said. Along the beach stretched an unpaved path, covered with white seashells. It led to a blue building that looked like a boathouse: the Chibineko Kitchen.

Outside the door, Mitsuyo could see an A-frame chalkboard that served as the restaurant's sign. 'Here we are,' Kotoko said, ushering Mitsuyo towards it. On the chalkboard were a few lines of white writing, accompanied by a picture of a kitten.

'Oh, how sweet!' said Mitsuyo. It wasn't a particularly skilful drawing, but it had clearly been done with love, and kindness seemed to emanate from the careful chalk lines.

'This is Chibi, the restaurant's cat,' Kotoko broke in, as though making a formal introduction. For a moment, Mitsuyo thought she was talking about the drawing. And then—

'*Miaow.*'

A kitten stuck its head out from behind the chalkboard. It was white with ginger patches, its face patterned just like the cat in the drawing.

The little cat was adorable enough to put a smile on anyone's face, but Kotoko frowned down at it. 'Didn't I just tell you you're not allowed outside?' She sighed. 'What will you do if a big scary crow decides to swoop down and pick on you? You could get hurt.'

The girl was obviously trying to sound stern, but the kitten didn't seem in the least intimidated.

'He must have sneaked out again,' Kotoko said to Mitsuyo.

The cat was a habitual escapee, then. Sora had never tried to get out of the house, but this kitten looked more mischievous. Mitsuyo thought he was a darling, but she could see why he would worry his owners. It would be dangerous out here for a pet cat.

Kotoko looked at Chibi. 'Do you understand? You've *got* to stay inside from now on,' she repeated.

'*Miaow*,' the kitten retorted, before trotting off towards the door, not looking at all sorry.

'Honestly . . .' Kotoko sighed again, and then she composed herself and scooted past Chibi to hold open the door. 'Thank you very much for making a reservation with us today, Mrs Yamada. Please come in.'

She was giving Mitsuyo a proper staff welcome to the restaurant. The only problem was that Chibi was in the way, walking unhurriedly over the threshold as though Kotoko was holding the door open just for him.

'Sorry about that,' said Kotoko, sheepishly.

'That's quite all right.' Mitsuyo smiled. What a delightful place this was.

She followed Chibi inside, where she was greeted by a young man with a kind face.

'Welcome to the Chibineko Kitchen, Mrs Yamada. My name is Kai Fukuchi. We've been waiting for you.'

It was the voice she had heard over the phone – the restaurant's owner, perhaps. A polite, handsome young man, wearing elegant glasses.

You weren't supposed to judge people based on appearances, she knew, but neither of the two looked like fraudsters. Yet nothing about them suggested any connection with death or the dead, either. They both seemed quiet – intellectual perhaps, Mitsuyo thought, the kind of people you might expect to find working in a city library.

'Will this seat be all right for you?' Kai said, showing her to a table by the window. Outside, the sea stretched away into the distance, and Mitsuyo could hear the waves and the cries of the black-tailed gulls.

'What a lovely restaurant,' she said. She meant it, and yet she realised she was feeling anxious again. It was so pleasant here, she was finding it harder and harder to believe that what she had heard about the place could be true.

The person Mitsuyo hoped to meet was not her husband or Sora, or even her long-dead parents.

She had come to see Ken'ichi Kawakubo, the late singer.

Mitsuyo had been born into a very ordinary family; there was no one among her relatives and friends, nor her neighbours, in the kind of profession where you might end up on television. So it might seem surprising that she had any sort of connection with the singer. But in fact they had met way back, around sixty years ago.

It wasn't really anything to boast about: Mitsuyo's parents had run a cheap, no-frills restaurant, and

Ken'ichi Kawakubo had dined there regularly before he became well-known.

Mitsuyo was a child at the time and her memories were a little hazy, but for some reason she could remember exactly what it was that Ken'ichi Kawakubo used to order. She had ordered the same dish for her remembrance meal.

'Please wait here for a moment and I will bring out your food.' Kai bowed like a waiter in a hotel restaurant, and then disappeared off into the kitchen.

Everything must have been prepared already, because just a few moments later Kai returned, carrying two large bowls of rice on a tray.

'Here you are,' he said, setting the bowls on the table, one in front of Mitsuyo and one at the place opposite. The second must be for Ken'ichi.

Mitsuyo could smell the tang of sweetened soy sauce. The fish that sat atop the rice looked like unagi, only it wasn't eel Mitsuyo had ordered – the eatery run by her family hadn't served anything so pricy.

'Your sardine kabayaki-don,' said Kai.

Yes, that was it – Mitsuyo's remembrance meal.

The sardine fishing industry had been thriving in Chiba Prefecture for several hundred years, and sardines were still one of the specialities of the region. They were supposed to be particularly delicious served raw as sashimi and garnished with grated ginger. In Mitsuyo's younger days, sardine had been the byword for cheap fish, but as the numbers caught had declined the price had risen, and now they could be considered a luxury.

Kai had cooked the sardines kabayaki style, with a sweet soy-sauce glaze. 'Although the fish I have used here is actually round herring, rather than true sardine.' Kai explained that the season for catching true sardines, or ma-iwashi, ran from May until October, whereas the similar urume-iwashi, or round herring, grew fatty between winter and early spring. As it was December, it was just getting to the time when the round herring were at their tastiest.

'Please enjoy.'

'Itadakimasu.' Mitsuyo put her hands together neatly and then picked up her chopsticks.

The flesh of the fish was tender and came apart easily. Underneath its sweet glaze, it looked very fresh. Lifting a piece to her mouth, she savoured the salty sweetness of the sauce, layered over the subtle flavour of the fish itself. Mitsuyo looked down at her bowl again, and saw that the white rice too was drenched in the sticky sauce. Her stomach rumbled. *How embarrassing*, she thought, flushing, but it looked so good she couldn't help it. She scooped some rice into her mouth, careful not to drop any, and the taste burst across her tongue.

Mitsuyo had never made sardine kabayaki herself, and she couldn't remember ever buying it in a bento box or ready-made in the shops, or eating it at a restaurant. Which would make it about fifty years since she'd last had it, cooked by her parents.

It tasted just as she remembered, and a wave of nostalgia washed over her. 'It's absolutely delicious,' she said quietly.

Only, her voice came out muffled.

That's strange.

She cleared her throat, but her cough sounded just as cloudy. Mitsuyo looked around, thinking she might ask for a glass of water, and then she noticed something else. Kai was gone. There was no sign of Kotoko, either. The two had been there only moments ago, she was sure of it, but now the little restaurant was empty.

'Hello . . .?' Mitsuyo whispered, but there was no reply. She began to grow anxious. Something very strange indeed was going on: when Mitsuyo looked out of the window, hoping to catch a glimpse of someone, she saw that the beach and the skies above it were empty.

No Kai. No Kotoko. Not even a solitary seagull.

Not every living thing had vanished, however. Chibi was still there, sitting on the rocking chair and gazing out of the window, unruffled.

'What's happening?' Mitsuyo asked the little kitten, panic in her voice.

Chibi gave a mew in reply that Mitsuyo could not interpret.

Mitsuyo looked around the restaurant once more. The pendulum of the old clock that stood next to the rocking chair had frozen mid-swing. In all her seventy years, she had never experienced anything like this before.

Mitsuyo was sitting there, completely at a loss, when suddenly, from outside the window, she heard the strains of a guitar. 'I know that song . . .'

As though in response to Mitsuyo's murmured words, a gentle voice floated in on the air. A familiar melody. It was 'Yesterday', by the Beatles. The song Paul McCartney had penned with his late mother in mind.

And the voice was that of Ken'ichi Kawakubo.

Was somebody listening to music out there? She turned to look out of the window again.

'No,' she gasped, unable to believe her eyes. Out on the beach, where she was quite sure there had been nothing before, there now stood a little wooden building.

Not only that, Mitsuyo knew it well.

'East Village . . .' she murmured, wonderingly.

That was the name of a little music venue on the edge of Shinjuku. Ken'ichi Kawakubo had played there often. But that couldn't be right! The place had been demolished not long after Ken'ichi had died, and she hadn't heard anything about it being rebuilt – and anyway, the building before her now looked at least a decade old. And the place hadn't even *been* there when Mitsuyo had arrived at the restaurant; it had appeared out of nowhere.

'What should I do . . .?'

'*Miaow*,' came Chibi's reply. As Mitsuyo glanced back at the kitten her gaze was drawn to the sardine kabayaki-don at the place opposite her, and she remembered what Kaburaki had told her in the hospital.

There's this restaurant where they say you can meet someone who's dead.

And here she was.

'Surely not . . .'

Mitsuyo finally understood what was happening. She had come to meet Ken'ichi. She had eaten the

140

remembrance meal. And now here, on this remote beach, was the venue she had seen him play at so many times.

Her hesitation gone, Mitsuyo stood up, walked over to the door of the Chibineko Kitchen and opened it.

And there stood East Village. It was built as she remembered it, of stacked timbers, like a log cabin, with a sign hanging on the door that said 'We are open'.

It was then that Mitsuyo realised that the beach was blanketed in a thick fog. All she could make out was the building before her.

The past came flooding back.

Mitsuyo had visited East Village more times than she could count.

The first time she went, she was in senior high school. She had gone with her parents, at her mother's request. En route to the little venue, her mother had been excited, happy. But Mitsuyo had noticed tears in her father's eyes.

Her mother was very ill. She had been discharged from hospital briefly, but in three days' time she would be going back in, and she was unlikely to come out again. They all knew it, including Mitsuyo's mother.

She had come home to spend her last days with her family.

'I want to hear some singing,' Mitsuyo's mother had said to her husband and daughter. She loved music and always had the radio on when she was busy in the kitchen. She wanted to go to a concert just once before she died. 'I want to listen to some wonderful live music with my family – then I'll be able to say I had a happy life.'

Her mother had been acting as though her life were already over, and Mitsuyo remembered how her father, usually so full of swagger, had cried and cried. She had cried too. It was only her mother who had smiled; in high spirits, she had decided where they would go. 'I'd like to see our Ken'ichi perform,' she said.

Ken'ichi Kawakubo had been a regular at their restaurant in the years before it had gone out of business, a short while before her mother's illness was discovered. He lived in the neighbourhood, so they knew he was a singer. He wasn't a successful one, however, earning his living as a day labourer and busking outside train stations and in parks.

And then, just as her parents' restaurant was failing, Ken'ichi Kawakubo had begun to appear on television now and again, and gained a little fame. He never did come out with a huge hit, but you occasionally heard him on the radio. He had such a gentle singing voice, it was hard to imagine him working as a day labourer, earning cash in hand.

'Listening to Ken'ichi sing makes me so happy,' Mitsuyo's mother had always said. She crooned along with him, out of tune but joyful, whenever his songs came on the radio.

Mitsuyo couldn't remember exactly how it had all come about, only that the three of them had set off for East Village as a family. She couldn't recall what Ken'ichi had sung that night, either. She had a feeling he might have performed 'Yesterday', but she couldn't be sure. She had found in her old age that even treasured memories grew hazy. What she did remember were her mother's words, whispered in her ear too quietly for her father to hear.

'Thank you for such a wonderful life.'

At that point, Mitsuyo remembered breaking down and sobbing. She had been trying to hold back her tears, at least during the show, but it had been hopeless. Her mother, a little dismayed, had stroked Mitsuyo's head, her hand gentle and warm.

Three days later, Mitsuyo's mother returned to hospital. She had taken the radio in with her and listened to music until her death a few months later. Despite the pain she must have felt, she was always smiling.

Perhaps it was for her mother's sake that Mitsuyo continued to listen to Ken'ichi Kawakubo's songs. And so she had gone to East Village time and time again, sometimes with her father, sometimes with friends – and, after they had met and got married, with her husband, too.

Before long she gave birth to a daughter. But then Mitsuyo's father had become ill.

Medicine had come a long way since Mitsuyo was a child, and it was common for a doctor to be able to say, with some accuracy, how long the patient had left. Mitsuyo's father seemed to have been expecting his prognosis. On the day the doctor confirmed that his condition was terminal, he said to Mitsuyo: 'Now, I hope you won't mind if I take a leaf out of your mother's book. I want to go and listen to some music with you.'

Mitsuyo wished there was something she could do to save him, but she knew it was impossible.

'Your mother will be with us too,' her father had continued. He carried a photograph of his late wife on his person at all times. It was the black-and-white picture of her he had been given before the two were formally introduced. In it, Mitsuyo's mother was gazing shyly at the camera, younger than Mitsuyo herself.

They had gone to East Village together to hear Ken'ichi Kawakubo sing. And when in the taxi, on the way home, Mitsuyo's father had said to her, 'I want you to be happy, now,' Mitsuyo had struggled to reply through her tears.

Her father went into the same hospital as his late wife, and there he died, the black-and-white photograph of her propped up at his bedside.

Now they were a family of three: Mitsuyo, her kind, quiet husband, and their daughter. There had been plenty of arguments and hardships, of course, but all in all, Mitsuyo thought, they had been happy. Ken'ichi Kawakubo's rendition of 'Yesterday' always played in her head as she dwelled on those memories. It really did seem as though everything had happened only yesterday.

But that was all in the past now. Mitsuyo's daughter had got married and gone to live in a town far away. Her gentle husband was gone too, and so was Ken'ichi. Even her Sora had left her behind.

*

'I've ended up all alone . . .' Mitsuyo murmured as she stood in the thick mist outside East Village. A tear trickled down her cheek as grief washed over her. But now wasn't the time for crying. Ken'ichi Kawakubo was on the other side of the building's closed door. He was right there, singing 'Yesterday'.

Mitsuyo wiped away her tears and pushed open the door.

The singing grew louder as she stepped inside the little music house that she knew no longer existed. And there he was, sitting on a chair, strumming away at his guitar. Ken'ichi was in his later years, his hair completely white, wearing round glasses. He looked exactly as she had seen him at his last concert, exactly as she had pictured him the moment she had heard that voice.

But not everything was as she had imagined. There were no other concert-goers in the little venue, and no staff. Only him.

The sign on the door had said they were open, but perhaps she wasn't meant to be in here—?

Ken'ichi, noticing her, paused in his playing. She thought he might be angry, and was about to apologise and leave when he said: 'I haven't seen you for a long time.'

The words took her by surprise. She was still casting around for a reply when he spoke again.

'You were at the restaurant, weren't you?' he said.

'What?'

'It is you, isn't it? The young lady from that restaurant by the train station? Fifty years ago now, it must be.'

'Y—yes,' Mitsuyo stammered. He remembered her! She couldn't believe it – but Ken'ichi wasn't finished.

'And you came to my concerts often, didn't you?'

Mitsuyo was speechless. She could only stand there, wide-eyed.

'Are you sure you wouldn't rather have met someone else?' Ken'ichi said.

She understood at once what he was asking. Kaburaki had told her that you only got one miracle. By choosing to summon Ken'ichi, she had given up her chance of seeing anyone else who had passed away.

'Yes. It's all right,' she replied, nodding.

Mitsuyo longed to see her mother again, her father, her husband. Sora, too. If she had been a few years younger, perhaps she would have chosen one of them instead. But she was seventy now, and the end of her life was beginning to come into view. She would see her family again when she passed into the next world; she was certain they would be waiting for her. But Ken'ichi Kawakubo was just an acquaintance, almost a stranger. She didn't think she would have another chance to meet him there.

And so she was able to answer him unequivocally: 'It was you I wanted to see.'

Mitsuyo sat in the front row of the empty audience seats, and Ken'ichi Kawakubo resumed his song.

She found herself instantly soothed. Old people with no tomorrow like songs about yesterdays; they bring back happy memories. Memories of helping out in her parents' restaurant. Picnics with her mother and father. Being introduced to the man she would later marry, and going on their first date together. Her father's face, streaked with tears on her wedding day. Her daughter's birth, and the time she first called Mitsuyo 'Mummy'. And then her own husband's face wet with tears on the day of their daughter's wedding. Their daughter and son-in-law taking them on holiday to a hot spring. The day Sora joined the family.

There had been plenty of hard times, Mitsuyo knew, but she remembered only the good. *It's been a wonderful life. I couldn't have asked for anything more.*

Ken'ichi Kawakubo played the last lingering notes of the beautiful, famous melody. Mitsuyo found herself too moved to even applaud, but Ken'ichi must have been able to see how much the music had touched her. 'I haven't sung anything in this world for so long. I was awfully nervous,' he said shyly.

This caught Mitsuyo's attention.

'You mean, you're still singing in the next world?'

'Yes. It's the only thing I know how to do,' Ken'ichi answered, as though it were the most natural thing there could be. 'I give concerts, too.'

'Really?' Mitsuyo was astonished.

'Yes, of course. At East Village in the world beyond.'

Mitsuyo imagined her parents and her husband making their way to one of Ken'ichi Kawakubo's concerts. Her husband would be clasping Sora in his arms, smiling brightly.

But there was no Mitsuyo in the picture. She was the only one left out.

'Couldn't I come too?' she blurted out. And she meant it – she wanted to leave this life behind as soon as possible.

Ken'ichi was silent for a little while, and then he said, 'There's no hurry. You'll get there sooner or later.'

149

Mitsuyo knew what he meant. Everyone dies in the end. But suddenly she couldn't bear the waiting. 'I don't want to go back to an empty house,' she replied, simply.

Mitsuyo felt she couldn't be alone for a single day more. People lived so long nowadays, but that didn't mean one spent more time happy; it only meant one spent more time alone. Every evening, when she went to bed, Mitsuyo feared what would happen if she died in her sleep and nobody realised. She had no one to wish goodnight. And when morning came after all, the only thing she had to occupy her time was her occasional visits to the rehabilitation centre. Nobody needed her. No one would miss her. It wasn't just the paranoia of old age talking – it was simple fact. She often went entire days without speaking to anyone.

'It's no life. I might as well be dead. So I just want it to be over,' she said now, and a tear rolled down her cheek. She had never expected that getting old would be this wretched.

'That's not true,' said Ken'ichi Kawakubo. He stepped towards her, as if to comfort her. 'You're *living*, after all. I don't believe that you might as well be dead.'

It was what Mitsuyo had expected him to say. She had allowed herself the outburst because she wanted

Ken'ichi to reassure her. She flushed with embarrassment at herself, and yet she couldn't stop her tears. They seemed to come so easily now that she was old.

But she didn't want to bore Ken'ichi with her tears; she had that much self-awareness left, at least. 'I'm sorry, I'll stop – please keep playing,' she said, forcing cheerfulness into her voice. She wanted to hear Ken'ichi sing again, to sink back into her memories.

Dying wouldn't be so difficult, she thought; she could manage it by herself . . . 'Please, sing another one,' Mitsuyo implored again, bowing her head.

But Ken'ichi didn't resume playing. Mitsuyo looked up at him. His gaze was still kind, but he had put the guitar down. *He must be fed up of playing for a weepy old woman.* She had ruined this magical concert.

'I'm so sorry. Please – just let me hear you play a little longer,' she said.

But some things can't be fixed with an apology; Mitsuyo's life was made up of many such regrets and missed opportunities.

'My song is done.' Ken'ichi's voice was gentle but firm, as though simply stating a fact.

'Done?' Mitsuyo said desperately. 'But—'

'It's time for me and East Village to return to the other world.'

'You're leaving?'

'Yes. I can only stay until the remembrance meal grows cold.'

This came as a shock to Mitsuyo. She hadn't realised – she hadn't even thought about it. She had forgotten about the food entirely. She'd been so busy feeling sorry for herself, she'd wasted precious time. She could weep all she wanted, but she would never get these moments back again.

Remembering the past didn't change the present, either.

Mitsuyo sat there, overwhelmed by the brutal passage of time. And then from out of nowhere she heard the mew of a cat.

'*Miaow.*'

It sounded like the late Sora. The cat had always called to Mitsuyo incessantly whenever she was out of sight.

She opened her mouth to reply, and then the world went dark.

It lasted only for a moment, and then light flooded back.

In that instant, the world returned to normal. Where only moments before Mitsuyo had been in East Village, now she was back in the Chibineko Kitchen, sitting in her seat by the window.

But not everything was quite as it had been. She could see Chibi, but there was still no Kai or Kotoko. Instead, Ken'ichi Kawakubo sat opposite her.

Mitsuyo looked at the old grandfather clock and saw that the pendulum remained motionless. She felt certain it wasn't broken, but that time itself had stopped.

The remembrance meal on the table was cooling, its steam barely visible now.

'Thank you very much for coming to see me.' Ken'ichi Kawakubo bowed his head. He was already starting to disappear, fading like an old photograph. He was returning to the world beyond.

Take me with you! I don't want to go on living alone! Mitsuyo wished with all her heart, but she didn't voice it this time.

Ken'ichi Kawakubo, however, seemed to know what she was thinking. 'You can't pass on to the next world yet. You still have things left to do in this one.'

Hadn't he listened to anything she had been saying? 'There's nothing left for me here,' Mitsuyo replied, frustrated.

'Yes, there is,' he said assuredly, as though he knew something she didn't.

Mitsuyo felt a glimmer of hope, and she caught her breath.

But Ken'ichi's next words were a joke. 'You've got to tell them all how good my music is.'

At first, Mitsuyo thought she hadn't heard him correctly. Then she felt a surge of anger. Tell *who* how good his music was? He was laughing at her, making fun of an old woman who was all on her own. He had been kind to her up until now, it was true, but Ken'ichi Kawakubo was an entertainer after all. He had probably never known what it was to be lonely.

I should never have come here, Mitsuyo thought, fiercely. Now her precious memories had been tarnished. He had even made a mockery of her parents, who had gone to listen to him sing at the end of their lives.

'I don't have anyone to tell,' she replied, coldly.

Ken'ichi must have been able to see that she was angry, yet he persisted with his joke. 'Yes, you do. Your friends,' he said.

He really *was* being cruel to her. And with this realisation, Mitsuyo's anger leached away, to be replaced by a deep sadness.

It was then that Chibi gave a little mew.

'*Miaow.*'

His voice was bright, and it sounded as though he was laughing.

Even the kitten was making fun of her now.

'Here they are now,' Ken'ichi said, as though interpreting for Chibi.

'What?' said Mitsuyo. But her confusion lasted only moments: before Ken'ichi could reply, she heard voices from outside the window.

'Mrs Yamada, are you in there?'

'We've come to get you, Mitsuyo!'

'If you're there, come on out!'

Surprised, she recognised the three voices immediately: it was the coffee-morning folk from the rehabilitation centre.

Mitsuyo looked out of the window and saw that East Village had vanished without a trace. There was the white seashell path she had followed to get here, and there were the faces she knew.

'It's Fujii and Tomomi – and Kanayama, too . . .'

The three of them were glaring at the door to the restaurant, looking as though they were about to force their way in.

'What are they doing here?' Mitsuyo whispered.

'You missed today's coffee morning, so I gather they got worried and went round to your house,' Ken'ichi said. That made sense: they all sent each other New Year's cards, and the three had attended her husband's funeral, too, so they knew where Mitsuyo lived. 'But you weren't in. You were already on the train by then.'

They had wanted to phone her, Ken'ichi told Mitsuyo, but they didn't know her mobile number, and the staff at the rehabilitation centre wouldn't give out her personal information. 'They suspected right away that you had gone off somewhere dangerous.'

That somewhere dangerous would be the Chibineko Kitchen. They had all got it into their heads that the restaurant was some sort of den of vice.

'And so they decided to come and rescue you,' said Ken'ichi.

As it was Kaburaki who had told Mitsuyo about the Chibineko Kitchen, she realised that Fujii or one of the others might have visited him in hospital and heard about it there too.

Old people are always the worst busybodies, for ever getting the wrong end of the stick and letting themselves get carried away. But what had they planned to do if this place actually had been dangerous? And coming all the way out here, too – it was reckless behaviour!

'Well, you went to see Kaburaki in hospital. That was a long way, too,' said Ken'ichi.

'But that's different . . .' said Mitsuyo.

'Is it?' he asked, simply. 'It's normal to care about your friends.'

'Friends?' Mitsuyo echoed, and then she remembered what he had said earlier: *You've got to tell them all how good my music is.*

So Ken'ichi hadn't been making fun of her. Mitsuyo had misunderstood. She'd been so busy yearning for the old days, she hadn't realised she had friends in the present.

For so long now, she had been living her life facing backwards.

She wasn't alone after all. Ken'ichi Kawakubo had shown her that she wasn't alone; that she had friends who called her by her name.

She looked back to the table to thank him, but Ken'ichi was nowhere to be seen. He had returned to the other world.

'Thank you,' Mitsuyo said anyway, and bowed her head before the remembrance meal. It was no longer steaming. Her voice came out clearly now. The miracle was over.

The pendulum of the old grandfather clock resumed its swing.

The next thing Mitsuyo knew, Kai and Kotoko were standing by her table. She didn't think either of them had seen Ken'ichi.

Kai looked out of the window at Fujii and the others. 'Are they acquaintances of yours, Mrs Yamada?'

There was only one answer Mitsuyo could give. 'They're my dear friends,' she said, and Chibi gave a happy '*Miaow*.' Of course – she wasn't the only who had met Ken'ichi Kawakubo: the kitten had followed her into that hazy world too, and had seen everything that had happened to her.

'In that case, allow me to show them in,' said Kai.

Kotoko went to brew tea for four. The remembrance meal was cleared away and new places set and, as if by magic, the restaurant was ready to welcome in Mitsuyo's friends.

Mitsuyo was prepared for their inevitable questions. She felt that if she explained, she could get them to understand.

She was sure they would come to appreciate Ken'ichi Kawakubo's music, too. People often lived to a hundred these days, so they had plenty of time.

'D'you reckon we should call the police?' she heard Fujii say from outside.

'Yes, I think so,' came Kanayama's low voice.

158

'Right – I'll do it now.' That was Tomomi.

Kotoko opened her eyes wide in surprise at this alarming development.

'I'd better be quick,' Kai said as if to himself, and started for the door – but Mitsuyo called him back.

'Wait, please. I'll show them in myself,' she said. Her coffee-morning acquaintances had come ready for a showdown. It wasn't fair to put Kai in the firing line, and besides, Mitsuyo wanted to greet them herself.

'Certainly,' Kai said, and held open the door for her. Chibi looked eagerly towards the beach, but Kotoko scooped him up. From her arms, the kitten gave a disappointed mew.

Mitsuyo rose from her chair and went outside.

The light was dazzling and she could smell salt on the breeze. The vastness of sea and sky stretched out before her.

Mitsuyo called out to her three busybody friends.

'Here I am!'

A special recipe from the
Chibineko Kitchen

Iwashi no Kabayaki-don:

Soy-glazed sardines on rice

Ingredients (serves 2)

- 4 fresh whole sardines (or pre-butterflied fillets)
- A pinch of salt
- Flour (enough to coat the fish)
- Sesame oil, for frying
- Approx 2 tbsp each of cooking saké, mirin, soy sauce, sugar
- 2 portions of rice

Method

1. If using whole sardines, remove the heads and guts, butterfly the fish by hand and remove the backbones.
2. Sprinkle salt on both sides of the fillets, set aside for

3 minutes and then wipe off any moisture with kitchen roll.

3. Coat the sardines in flour.

4. Heat the sesame oil in a pan and fry the sardines skin-side down. When they have browned, turn them over and fry the other side.

5. Combine the saké, mirin, soy sauce and sugar, adjusting to taste, and pour the mixture into the pan with the sardines.

6. Continue to cook for around 2 minutes until the sardines are well coated in the sauce.

7. Serve in large bowls on top of rice.

Tips

This dish can also be made with fish such as Pacific saury (sanma) or horse mackerel (aji). Garnish with chopped shiso leaves or other toppings if desired.

4

A calico cat and yesterday's curry

三島湖

Mishima Lake

Mishima Lake is the perfect place to appreciate the beauty of the changing seasons. In spring the forest on its banks is fresh and green; trees burst into leaf and cherry blossom appears. In autumn the red leaves are mirrored on the surface of the water. The area around the lake and dam has been designated a twentieth-century heritage site, a haven to pass on to future generations of Kimitsu locals. The 3200 hectares of forest which surround Mishima Lake and the neighbouring Toyofusa Lake are known as the 'People's Springtime Forest', and visitors flock there every year to enjoy fishing, camping and walking.

Kimitsu City

Kumagai was the leader of the theatre company to which Kotoko belonged. His bear-like, bearded face made him appear to be in his forties, when in fact he was only a few years past thirty.

Though he confined himself to writing scripts for the group and never performed himself, during rehearsals he would sometimes demonstrate techniques to the other actors. Every time Kotoko watched him act, she remembered her late brother Yuito's words: 'I reckon you could call Kumagai a genius.'

Her brother had been proud and competitive, but he had spoken of Kumagai's talent with open admiration. Despite having been dubbed by magazines as a rising star himself, Yuito hadn't seemed to consider his talent a match for Kumagai's.

Kumagai could have held his own, everyone agreed, against any of the successful actors seen in leading roles on the stage and screen. Yet he never did any auditions.

'Why don't you act with us?' Kotoko often asked him, but he would never give her a proper answer, usually just fobbing her off with an, 'Oh, I don't know.'

When Kotoko had looked him up online, she had come across a few short news articles. There was one from around ten years ago, introducing him as an up-and-coming young talent. In the photo that accompanied the article he was beardless, and his classical good looks made Kotoko think of a Hollywood star. The article said he had a lot of young female fans, too.

But Kotoko didn't know what had happened to his career after that, and scouring the internet for more details would have felt like prying. She thought about asking him, but the days went by without the right moment occurring.

Then, one evening after rehearsal, as Kotoko was about to head home, Kumagai called her back. 'Have you got a minute?'

This wasn't unusual. Kotoko was a complete beginner to theatre – she would have blushed to call herself an actress – so she assumed Kumagai just wanted to give her a little extra coaching. The other members of the company must have thought the same, and they left Kumagai and Kotoko alone in the empty rehearsal hall.

'I have a favour to ask you,' Kumagai said. 'It's about the Chibineko Kitchen.'

It wasn't what Kotoko had expected. She had told Kumagai she was working at the restaurant part-time, but he had never asked her anything about it before, let alone come to visit.

'Oh yes?' she said.

'I want to request a remembrance meal this Sunday.'

Kumagai's words took Kotoko by surprise – but then again, he was the one who had told her about the Chibineko Kitchen in the first place. He had been there often in the past and he knew about the remembrance meals, too, so it wasn't so strange for him to decide to visit the restaurant. Only it wasn't Kotoko's job to take reservations: Kai took care of that.

Kumagai already seemed aware of this. 'Could you ask Kai for me?' he said. 'It would be a huge help. You can tell him everything he needs to know about me, can't you?'

'Well . . .' Kotoko hesitated. To prepare the meals in memory of guests' lost loved ones, the restaurant required some information before they could cook the food. It would be better if Kumagai just spoke to Kai directly, she thought – but Kumagai persisted.

'I knew Kai's mother, Nanami, well, but I've never properly spoken to Kai. I don't know how easy it would be to explain myself over the phone.'

Clearly his story was a difficult one to share, especially with people he didn't know. Kotoko got the sense that there was some weighty reason behind Kumagai's request, and her feeling of reluctance only grew – but Kumagai didn't wait for her answer.

'I want to meet my dead son,' he said.

'What?' Kotoko blurted out. *His dead son?* She hadn't even known he was married.

Kumagai barrelled on: 'Can you make a reservation for me and my ex-wife? Please. We want to see our boy.'

And that was how Kotoko learned about Kumagai's past.

Kumagai had belonged to a theatre company since he was a child; all his young life he had believed that his future lay in films and television.

He did well academically, but he had no desire to go to university. So when he graduated from senior high school he signed up to a talent agency. It was a major one, a household name, and it seemed like the fastest route to the career he had set his heart on.

In no time at all he had been cast in a TV drama on the NHK channel, albeit in a minor role. Kumagai was sure that if his performance went down well, then film work would follow. Everything was going to plan.

That was when he met her. Sumire Hayashibara.

Sumire was four years older than Kumagai, an actress represented by the same agency. Though not particularly famous, she knew exactly how to hold an audience. Kumagai fell head over heels in love with her.

And he was delighted when he discovered that she felt the same way about him. Kumagai proposed to Sumire without hesitation, their decision to get married seeming the most natural thing in the world.

When Kumagai turned twenty, they submitted their marriage papers to the local government office, afterwards sneaking into an empty rehearsal hall and making their own private wedding vows to each other.

'I will love you in sickness and in health, till death do us part,' Kumagai promised.

When they went in to tell the agency their good news the next day, they never thought for one moment that they might have to keep quiet about their marriage. Surely it would be a cause for celebration.

But: 'Is this some kind of joke? You're to split up *immediately*!' their boss at the agency had screamed at them.

Kumagai felt more shocked than angry. He and Sumire loved each other. Why should they have to separate?

'You really don't get it?' came the incredulous reply.

Kumagai really didn't, and he said so.

'Because *the public will go off you*,' the agency boss told him, in a tone that made it clear he felt he shouldn't have to spell it out.

Kumagai understood what his boss was saying, but he thought the agency must have misconstrued something. It was only pop idols whose popularity took a hit when they got married. That stuff had nothing to do with serious actors, or so he believed.

But it was Kumagai who had misunderstood. As a young actor who had only just turned twenty, the image being demanded of him was exactly that of an idol – none of the people involved in his career thought of him as a serious actor.

It was Sumire who bore the brunt of their boss's anger. He hurled abuse at her in front of everyone. 'You've got some nerve, sinking your claws into a promising new talent when your own career's going nowhere! Don't you understand your position here? You want a man, find one somewhere else!'

Sumire hung her head and said nothing, but Kumagai couldn't stay silent. 'There's *no* need to speak to her like that!'

'No? How should I speak to her then? Should I call her what she is – a cat in heat?'

Before Kumagai knew it he had lunged towards the man. He didn't hit him, just gave him a slight shove. But the agency boss had fallen to the ground exaggeratedly, scattering papers from his desk for added effect.

Everyone in the office was looking over at them. The man glared up at Kumagai from the floor. 'You think you're ever going to work in TV again?' he said, in a low voice.

Kumagai was promptly informed of his dismissal. The agency had a lot of clout within the industry, and once word got around that he had been violent, the casting calls dried up.

Sumire fared no better, shunned for having made a grab at a rising star whom the agency had been taking special care to cultivate. Almost overnight, the two were exiled from the world of show business.

Their life together went on, and before long they had a child – a boy they named Shoma. Things weren't easy. They put their son into nursery, and both Kumagai and Sumire worked hard to make ends meet. Kumagai found a job at a removal company, carrying boxes from morning till night, quickly forgetting that he had ever been an actor.

Children grow rapidly, and in what seemed like no time at all, Shoma had started primary school. He was the spitting image of Kumagai as a boy, and precocious. He was a cheeky kid, Kumagai thought affectionately, but maybe that was normal for children his age nowadays.

Unfortunately, Kumagai and Sumire's time off rarely overlapped. Sumire's department store shifts kept her busy at weekends and on public holidays, so her days off hardly ever coincided with the school's. The couple hadn't wanted their young child spending all that time without them, so Kumagai tried to be home at the weekends, whenever work allowed.

Today was one of those days. Father and son waved Sumire off to work, and then Kumagai said, 'Want to go out somewhere?'

'Yeah!' Shoma replied.

They lived in a small town in Chiba Prefecture, as it was cheaper than renting a flat in Tokyo. They could have moved further away, but somehow it was hard to leave Tokyo behind completely. While Kumagai told himself he had moved on from his acting days, perhaps he still couldn't quite let go.

Chiba was home to Disneyland but Shoma hadn't shown any interest in going there. He loved the outdoors, and preferred fishing and camping to theme parks.

'Can we go and see a hand-dug tunnel?' he asked now.

It was a surprising request for a primary-school child to make. Kumagai had never even heard of hand-dug tunnels before moving to this town, but they were notable sights on the Boso Peninsula. The old tunnels, cut through mountainsides, weren't shored up with concrete but had been left bare inside, leaving the layers of rock exposed. Shoma was fascinated by them.

'They're so cool! Come on, Dad, let's go and see one!' he would pester Kumagai. Strangely enough, he never expressed a desire to go with Sumire. When Kumagai asked Shoma about this, he had replied, in a serious voice: 'Because it's a manly adventure. Mum wouldn't like it, she'd get bored.'

It sounded like something he'd picked up from a manga or an anime. Every time Sumire heard the words 'manly adventure' she burst out laughing.

On this particular day, Kumagai and Shoma planned their outing based on information they found online. Their destination was the hand-dug tunnel next to Mishima Lake in Kimitsu.

It was Shoma who had come across it. 'Look, it looks awesome!' he had said, holding up his phone to show Kumagai a set of photos taken at Mishima Dam.

'Seems like a beautiful place,' said Kumagai.

'Yeah. And it says now is the best time to visit.'

It was December – a time when the reds and yellows of the remaining autumn leaves, mingling with the deep colours of the evergreen trees, were reflected in the still water of the reservoir.

'Let's go, and then if it's good, we can take Mum next time,' Shoma said.

Kumagai smiled at this. For all his cheekiness, and his talk of 'manly adventures', his son was considerate of his mother too.

'Good plan,' Kumagai had replied, as they got into the little car he had bought on hire purchase.

That was when he had still thought there would be a next time.

As they had got closer to Mishima Lake, the traffic on the roads increased. It was a sunny Sunday, and lots of day trippers seemed to be heading in the same direction.

Kumagai worried that all the lunch spots might be full. 'Shall we eat first?' he asked his son.

'Okay.'

They slowed down when they spotted a family-friendly restaurant by the side of the road. It was still early and there was plenty of space in the car park. Outside the restaurant was a banner advertising a special curry menu.

'I'd rather have your curry, though, Dad,' Shoma said when he saw it.

'Oh yeah?'

'Yeah. It's on a whole other level,' Shoma said with great confidence, despite never having had curry at a family restaurant before.

These moments were entirely ordinary: Kumagai had had the same sort of conversation with Shoma yesterday, and the day before, and expected to do the same tomorrow.

He had forgotten that all things come to an end.

Kumagai pulled in, parking the little car in a space close to the entrance. 'Right, out you get,' he said to Shoma.

'Okay.'

They had both unclipped their seatbelts and were about to open their doors when, out of nowhere, a car came hurtling towards them.

The whole thing was over in an instant, yet Kumagai would always remember every little detail. The face of the grey-haired man behind the wheel of the oncoming car. The moment the car rammed into them, on the side where Shoma was sitting. Their own car rocking as though they had been caught in a major earthquake. The red creeping across his view.

Kumagai groaned. He raised a hand to his forehead; it was blood trickling from a cut that had clouded his vision. But he didn't spare a thought for his own injuries. 'Shoma, are you all right?'

There was no reply. Shoma was no longer in the passenger seat.

Kumagai instantly panicked, not knowing what to do; he only knew he needed to see his son. 'Shoma! *Shoma!*' he shouted frantically, only then realising that Shoma had slipped from his seat down into the footwell.

'Shoma!' Kumagai yelled so hard he thought his throat would tear.

But Shoma didn't answer. He just lay there, motionless. He didn't seem to be bleeding, but his neck was twisted at an unnatural angle, like a broken doll.

'Shoma, Shoma . . .' Kumagai's voice grew quieter. He tried to call out again, but no sound came.

He might have lost consciousness, he couldn't really remember from that point on. From somewhere in the distance he could hear the sound of sirens.

*

'They told me the man had accidentally stepped on the accelerator instead of the brake.'

In the empty rehearsal hall, with the rest of the theatre company gone, Kumagai spoke in a low voice.

It was an all-too-common accident: the kind that was actually more liable to happen in car parks than out on the roads.

'By the time the ambulance arrived, it was too late,' Kumagai said.

'Oh . . .' Kotoko exhaled.

'He wasn't breathing. They said he died instantly.'

Just like my brother. Yuito too had been hit by a car, and had died before the ambulance arrived, right in front of Kotoko.

She felt the urge to scream just remembering it, and tears burned her eyes.

And now Kotoko understood. She saw, clearly, why it was that she kept returning to the Chibineko Kitchen. She had been drawn to the job by Kai, there was that – but, somehow, working there was helping to heal the wound. Each time she journeyed back and forth to the town by the sea, the pain receded just a little.

'Sorry to make more work for you – but let me know if I can make a reservation,' Kumagai said, and with that, he left the room.

Kotoko reached for her phone and pulled up Kai's number.

Kumagai was heading for the Chibineko Kitchen, Kotoko having confirmed his reservation with him a few days earlier.

He had decided to go there on his motorbike instead of by train, as it was what he was used to.

As he sped along, Kumagai thought of Kotoko's brother. Yuito had been more than ten years his junior, but they had been good friends and, on days off, they had often gone touring along the coast. They'd visited the Chibineko Kitchen together, too.

Now all that was consigned to the past. To live was to watch second after second slip away – time that you could never get back again.

Being a Sunday, there was a lot of traffic on the road from Tokyo to Chiba. Plenty of families out and about. *Off to Disneyland, maybe.* Kumagai spotted a few elderly people behind the wheel, and seeing them sent his mind reeling back.

One and a half years in jail. That was the sentence given to the eighty-two-year-old man whose car had ploughed into theirs. Although the penalty sounded light, it was fairly standard. In cases where the offence didn't come under death by dangerous driving, the offender even often got off with a suspended sentence.

'He killed our son! He deserves the death penalty . . .' Sumire had said, again and again. Kumagai had said nothing, lacking even the energy to reply. Of course he resented, even hated, the driver, but more than that he hated himself for having failed to protect his Shoma.

He was full of regrets. *I should have taken a proper look around before letting him unclip his seatbelt. I shouldn't have taken him to that restaurant. We should have stayed at home and played games. I should never have bought such a small car. I should have died instead of him.*

He tried to ask his wife's forgiveness, but no words came. Apologising wouldn't bring back their child. Grovelling on his knees would change nothing.

There are things in this world that can never be undone.

When he looked in the mirror, he saw Shoma's features in his own, and pain stabbed his chest. Sumire cried every time she looked at him. Kumagai stopped shaving, but nothing could heal the hurt that lay between him and his wife. He couldn't stand to see Sumire suffering, but he had lost the energy he needed to support her in her grief.

The couple waited until a year after Shoma's death, and then they divorced.

When Kumagai had stamped his seal on the legal papers, he had felt fresh tears welling up. It was he who had suggested they separate – and yet he still loved Sumire.

After the divorce, Kumagai moved back to Tokyo.

To fill his empty days, he decided to start a theatre company. And so, keeping his full beard and hiding the fact that he used to be an actor, he established the group. Luckily it attracted a fair few members, and while Kumagai sometimes had to take on other work, one way or other he earned enough money to get by. But he could never explain, even to himself, why he only ever wrote scripts for the group, and never performed on stage.

His new life had begun, but not a day went by when he didn't think of Shoma, and he made several trips a month to the town by the sea to visit his son's grave.

The gravestone was always clean. Sumire must be visiting it, too; she had chosen to remain in Chiba.

At first Kumagai visited the grave alone, but later Yuito had begun to join him. He apparently knew a little about Kumagai's past from what he had seen

179

online: that Kumagai had been a TV actor, and that he had lost his son in a traffic accident.

'Would you let me light some incense at the grave?' Yuito had asked, and Kumagai had had no reason to refuse. He was touched that Yuito wanted to pray for Shoma's happiness in the next world.

A hush lay over the cemetery where Shoma was at rest. Many of the graves looked abandoned, and the place smelled of moss and damp earth. There were war graves, too, but Kumagai had never seen anyone praying at them.

It felt as though time had stopped, in this quiet cemetery. And it was there that Kumagai and Yuito had met Nanami Fukuchi.

They had caught sight of her a few times on their visits, and the three eventually introduced themselves to each other. 'I'm praying to the ancestors that my husband will come back,' Nanami told them. It was why she visited the grave so often: her husband had been missing at sea for more than fifteen years.

The law states that when a person is missing and it's not known whether they are dead or alive, after a certain period of time has elapsed they are treated as deceased. The period of absence is one year when the person has gone missing due to a particularly perilous event such as a war or a shipwreck, and seven years in all other ordinary cases.

Fifteen years far exceeded either. But Nanami hadn't lost hope. 'You probably think I'm being ridiculous, but I believe he'll come back,' she told Kumagai and Yuito.

She wasn't just strong in spirit, she was kind-hearted too, and she freely offered her prayers for Shoma. In turn, Kumagai and Yuito stood before the Fukuchi family grave and prayed that Nanami's husband would return.

Kumagai didn't know whether their prayers would be answered, but he pressed his hands together in earnest.

One day, after they had stood together for a while, Nanami said: 'I run a little restaurant about ten minutes' walk from here. Would you like to come and have something to eat?'

And that was how Kumagai and Yuito first discovered the Chibineko Kitchen.

Nanami had led them along the beach to the restaurant.

At the end of a path strewn with white seashells was a building that looked a little like a boathouse. There was no sign above the door, but a chalkboard stood beside it, and written there was the restaurant's name, followed by a curious statement:

We serve remembrance meals.

Kumagai and Yuito had stood wondering what this might mean, until Nanami explained: 'I make kagezen.'

That rang a bell. Kagezen was the food you offered up to pray for the safety of someone who had been absent for a long time. Sometimes, it was also the name given to the food prepared for the deceased at Buddhist funerals and memorials. Perhaps Nanami did funeral catering, Kumagai thought – but it turned out to be something else entirely.

'When you eat a remembrance meal at the Chibineko Kitchen, you can hear the voice of a loved one. Sometimes you can even speak to them,' she said.

'A loved one?' said Yuito.

'Somebody who's no longer in this world.'

'What?' Yuito said, astonished.

'You don't believe me?' said Nanami.

'I—no . . .'

'I don't blame you. It *is* unbelievable, isn't it? The idea of a dead person appearing,' Nanami said, almost apologetically. But she didn't sound as though she was lying, and Kumagai believed her.

Shoma's face rose to his mind, and the only thing that stopped him from requesting a remembrance meal there and then was the thought of Sumire. The miracle could only happen once, Nanami told them. If Kumagai went ahead, he would rob his wife of the chance of seeing their son again. And there was no guarantee that it would even happen. If he got Sumire's hopes up for nothing, he feared the shock of it might break her. Indeed, Kumagai didn't know whether he himself would be able to bear the disappointment.

Kumagai had visited the Chibineko Kitchen several times after that, but always put off ordering a remembrance meal. Then Yuito had been killed, hit by a car while saving his sister.

Kumagai had seen Kotoko at the Niki family grave, not long after the memorial service for the forty-ninth day since Yuito's death. She had seemed almost lifeless, her face ashen; she didn't look as though she was getting any food or sleep. Kumagai feared she would wreck herself if she carried on like that.

So he had told her about the remembrance meals at the Chibineko Kitchen, and then a true miracle had occurred – Kotoko had spoken to her late brother.

Kotoko had told Kumagai all about it during rehearsal, sometime later. She let him know that Nanami had died, too, and that Nanami's only son, Kai, had taken over the restaurant, and was continuing the tradition of serving remembrance meals.

Kumagai knew that the time had come to make a decision, before this chance slipped away from him. How many more years did he have left himself? He couldn't say. So he phoned his estranged wife.

Her number hadn't changed. Her voice, too, was achingly familiar. Kumagai was struck by a pang of nostalgia for their life together, but he said nothing of it, instead getting straight to the point: 'Will you come with me for a remembrance meal?'

'Yes. I'll come,' Sumire replied immediately.

She must have already heard about the Chibineko Kitchen, and Kumagai wondered whether she had met Nanami when she was visiting Shoma's grave, as he himself had done.

'No, I found out about it at the hospital,' Sumire told him.

'The hospital?'

'Yes. The one by the sea.'

Kumagai knew which she meant. It was a major hospital, the best in the prefecture, known for its excellent doctors. Many of the locals were born in that hospital, and spent their final days there, too.

'Are you all right?' Kumagai asked, concerned.

'Yes, I'm fine,' Sumire said. She sounded as though she was telling the truth. *Perhaps she just went in for a check-up,* Kumagai reassured himself, *or a vaccination. Something minor, anyway.*

The hospital waiting room was crowded with patients standing in line for their check-ups.

The long wait had tired Sumire out, and once her appointment was over she sat on a bench in the court-yard to rest, listening to the cries of the gulls and the shushing of the waves that told her the sea was close by. *I'll be forty soon,* she thought absently.

She was the only one sitting in the courtyard, but people passed by every now and again. Sumire was just about to get up and leave when a little girl of primary-school age walked by. As the child passed in front of her, she staggered all of a sudden.

'Are you all right?' Sumire jumped up and put her hands out to steady the girl. 'Just wait, I'll go inside and fetch someone.'

The girl was wearing pyjamas with a coat over the top; she must be an inpatient there. 'It's okay. It happens

185

a lot,' the girl reassured her in a steady voice, but Sumire couldn't help but wonder if she were just putting on a brave face.

Seeing other children always reminded Sumire of Shoma, and her eyes filled. Tears came to her so readily since Shoma's death that she was well-practised at holding them at bay. But she was feeling particularly sensitive that day, and she found she couldn't keep them from spilling over.

'What's wrong?' the girl asked in surprise, and Sumire realised that she had been waiting a long time for someone to ask her that. Perhaps she had needed to cry in front of someone else.

'Shoma's dead,' Sumire said simply, and the tears ran down her cheeks.

Sumire sat on the bench with the girl she'd only just met and told her about how her son had died. There was no one walking by anymore, and it hardly seemed like the same busy hospital. A hush had fallen, and a thin fog was creeping in from the sea.

'Lucky Shoma . . .' said the girl quietly, once Sumire had finished.

'What?' Sumire blurted out. The girl's response took her aback; she really did sound envious of Sumire's dead son. 'What do you mean, *lucky*?'

'Because he got to go to school, and go out on drives with his dad. And even though he's gone, look how much you're still crying for him.'

Sumire had no idea how to respond. Anger might have been justified, but she didn't sense any spite behind the girl's words.

The child went on matter-of-factly. 'I don't think I'll get to grow up, or even live long enough to go to junior high.'

Sumire sat in stunned silence. This girl, so very young, was facing her own death calmly, talking about it as though it were happening to someone else.

The girl told Sumire that her heart had been weak since birth and that she spent more time in hospital than she did at home. Though she had a satchel full of textbooks, she hadn't attended school even for a single day.

'I *am* scared of dying, but I'm only making things hard for my mum and dad,' the girl said.

If she died, things would be easier for her parents – was that what she meant? 'Of course you're not! You mustn't think that! You're not making things hard for them,' Sumire said in a rush, though she knew nothing about the girl's parents.

After falling silent for a few seconds, the girl replied: 'Thanks. You're a nice person.' And then, changing the subject, she told Sumire about the Chibineko Kitchen.

'The remembrance meals can bring back people who are gone from this world.'

It was impossible, what she was saying, and yet Sumire didn't think the girl was lying. She didn't seem to mind whether or not Sumire believed her.

'I have to go now.' The girl got up from the bench, and slowly walked away. Sumire found herself unable to call after her, so she just sat and watched her disappear into the mist.

The whole thing had felt utterly unreal.

Kumagai had arrived at the town by the sea. But to get to the Chibineko Kitchen he'd have to follow the path along the sandy beach, he knew, and he didn't want to attempt it on his motorbike.

Instead, he parked the bike in the car park in front of the station. He wasn't going to leave it out on the street. Kumagai followed the rules of the road almost neurotically now, the accident never far from his mind. Besides, he wanted to walk through this place again, the town where his son lay at rest.

He boarded an almost empty bus outside the station, and in ten minutes' time he was paying his fare and getting out by the Koitogawa. There was no one else around; it was so quiet, in fact, that he could hear the murmuring of the current.

He followed the river until Tokyo Bay came into view. Walking along the beach where the black-tailed gulls played, he came to the seashell path. The shells were as white as they always had been, giving the impression that the path was blanketed in snow.

The restaurant too, with its blue walls and its chalk-board, was unchanged, but when he got closer, he could see that the writing on the board was different.

'Of course . . . Nanami's not here anymore.' Kumagai felt a renewed sadness. It wasn't just Shoma who had been taken from him, but Nanami and Yuito, too. He gave a sigh, and opened the door to the restaurant.

'I'm Kumagai. I have a reservation,' he said – but when the reply came, it wasn't human.

'*Miaow.*'

There was the little white kitten with ginger patches, sitting daintily inside the doorway. *Chibi*. Kumagai remembered him from the last time he had visited.

Standing not far behind him was a young man wearing glasses.

'Welcome to the Chibineko Kitchen – we've been expecting you. My name is Kai Fukuchi,' he said with a polite bow.

Nanami's son. Kumagai had seen him helping in the restaurant in the past, but it was the first time Kai had greeted him like this.

Kumagai couldn't get used to the fact that Nanami was no longer there. It felt as though the restaurant he had been so fond of had become some other place. Pushing the thought away, Kumagai had just opened his mouth to greet the Chibineko Kitchen's new owner when he realised there was someone else there too.

'You're early,' she said.

It was Sumire. She was seated, wearing a loose-fitting dress, her gently waved brown hair tied back in a ponytail. She looked the tiniest bit plumper than he remembered.

'So are you,' Kumagai said.

He looked around the restaurant, but couldn't see Kotoko anywhere. Perhaps she had taken the day off so as not to intrude on his remembrance meal, or maybe she would be along later.

'This way, please.' Kai showed Kumagai to the seat next to Sumire. He waited for Kumagai to sit, and then promptly began: 'There is no guarantee you will be able to see the departed.' He spoke quietly but with emphasis, as though to make sure they understood this before he served the food. He told them, also, that he had never yet heard of the dead appearing to two people at once.

'That's all right,' Kumagai replied. There were no absolutes in life. Especially not when it came to something as unusual as this. 'We will accept whatever happens today.'

'We really appreciate it,' Sumire said, and bowed her head.

'Very good. Please wait just a moment and I will bring out your meal.' Kai withdrew to the kitchen. Without Kotoko here, he was presumably handling everything by himself.

'*Miaow.*' Chibi gave a short mew as though in response to Kai's words, and then jumped up onto the rocking chair next to the old grandfather clock. He gave a yawn, curled up into a ball and began to take slow, regular breaths.

Kumagai and Sumire were left alone together. They had no words to say to one another, and so they remained silent, listening to the sound of the waves outside, the cries of the gulls. The old clock was *tick-tock*ing away the seconds, too. There was nothing to occupy them, but they weren't restless. They just sat there in the quiet, not thinking of anything in particular.

It wasn't long before Kai returned, carrying a portable gas ring and a large, heavy pot. 'I will cook at the table, if I may,' he said. Putting the things down, he went back into the kitchen, and came back with a plate piled with seafood, meat and vegetables: prawns, clams, chicken thighs, pork belly, Chinese cabbage, chrysanthemum greens, shiitake mushrooms and carrots.

'It's yosenabe,' Sumire said.

Kumagai could tell by her voice that she was thinking fondly of days gone by. This was a dish everybody knew: a hotpot made with leftovers. There were no hard and fast rules about the ingredients, and it was easy to make. You brewed dashi stock from dried bonito flakes and kelp, set it boiling in an earthenware pot and then just added whatever you had in the kitchen. Sumire used to make yosenabe often, whatever the season.

Kai switched on the gas ring. He had already prepared the dashi, so all he needed to do was add the other ingredients to the pot. A moment's work and it was simmering away, sending up mouth-wateringly fragrant steam.

'May I serve it up when it's ready?' Sumire asked Kai, looking at the pot.

'Certainly,' said Kai, and he left them to switch off the gas ring themselves.

He seemed to prefer to give his guests space. *Not like Nanami*, Kumagai thought. She had always bustled around making sure everyone was being looked after.

'Let's eat,' Sumire said, and she dished some chicken, Chinese cabbage and chrysanthemum greens into Kumagai's bowl.

'Thank you.' She still remembered all the foods he liked best.

The two each placed their palms together formally, as if in prayer, just as they had always done when they had been a family of three.

'Itadakimasu.'

Kumagai tried the chicken first. It was firm but not tough, and when he bit into it the juices flowed out; the seafood and pork cooking alongside it in the pot had lent a depth to the flavour.

'It's good,' Kumagai heard himself murmur, and Sumire nodded.

'Mm, delicious. I can feel it warming me up.'

Kumagai looked across at the place opposite and saw that Sumire had set out a portion for Shoma, too. She had given him chicken, pork and vegetables.

A sad smile touched Kumagai's lips as memories came back to him. Shoma hadn't liked vegetables, and when they had yosenabe he would only ever help himself to the meat.

It had always been Sumire who scolded him – 'You've got to eat your greens too!' – while Kumagai had been the mediator: 'He'll start liking vegetables when he gets older. I was the same at his age, all I ever ate was meat.'

'You shouldn't spoil him. What if he gets ill?'

They'd had this conversation time and time again. Sumire had known she was being harsh, not really believing that Shoma would get seriously ill. She and Kumagai had been a young married couple, sickness and death far-off prospects.

They had certainly never imagined that their son would be dead before his tenth birthday; that he would be dead before they were.

Life was cruel. Kumagai pictured Shoma's face, his body crumpled in the footwell of the car. The chopsticks felt suddenly heavy in his hand. He quietly placed them down, and saw that Sumire had done likewise. Maybe it was the same memories that had driven away her appetite.

The hotpot was only half eaten. The steam was still

rising, but there was no Shoma. No miracle for Kumagai and Sumire.

There is no guarantee you will be able to see the departed, Kai had warned them.

The hopes of the estranged husband and wife turned to disappointment.

The gas had been left on all this time, and Kumagai was just reaching over to switch it off when Kai emerged from the kitchen and came unhurriedly over to the table.

The bits and pieces that remained in the hotpot were now overcooked and beginning to fall apart; it didn't look so appetising anymore. Kumagai assumed Kai had come to clear away the meal, but instead, he looked at the limp vegetables and said something unexpected.

'It's ready.'

'Ready?' Kumagai echoed, and Kai nodded.

'Yes. Cooking the vegetables until very well done can make them more palatable for those who are less keen on them.'

For a moment Kumagai was baffled.

'Wait, you mean—?' Sumire said.

And then Kumagai understood too. The yosenabe wasn't their remembrance meal; there was another dish that featured even more prominently in his memories. It was something he'd mentioned to Kotoko when he asked her to make the reservation, but for some reason it had gone clean out of his head.

He should have realised when he saw Kai leaving the hotpot to simmer that this was the meal he had always intended to make.

'Excuse me,' said the owner of the Chibineko Kitchen, as he leant over the table and spooned an aromatic sauce into the pot.

Kumagai caught a whiff of spice. Anyone from Japan would recognise what Kai was cooking now.

Kai stirred until the sauce was well mixed with the leftover yosenabe, and then he said to Kumagai and Sumire: 'Shime curry, to round off your hotpot.'

Curry is a favourite among children, and Shoma had been no exception. He would even tolerate vegetables if they were cooked in a curry. And so the family had eaten chicken curry and pork curry; curry topped with freshly fried katsu or breaded prawns; summer vegetable curry; autumn curry packed with mushrooms; miso curry with beef and aubergines; curry with loquat fruits, which were a Boso speciality; and, of course, shime curry – to finish up leftover hotpot.

Kumagai had first made the dish after seeing it prepared on a cooking show. The recipe couldn't be easier – it was just a matter of adding curry sauce to the remains of the hotpot and heating it through. It worked well with hotpots that included carrots and onions, but even things you wouldn't expect in a curry – burdock root, long green onions, chrysanthemum greens – were delicious when eaten this way.

Kumagai had liked to make the curry sauce from scratch, buying all the spices from the supermarket and blending them in different ways to make a whole variety of curries. It sounded as though Kai did the same: 'I've kept it mild, and classic Japanese style,' he said, adding a dash of soy sauce to finish. He set out helpings of rice, too, in large bowls rather than plates, the way they served curry on rice at soba-noodle restaurants: a dish to be eaten with chopsticks rather than a spoon.

Kumagai had made it just like this. The dish he had eaten so many times with his family, the family that was now lost to him, was right there in the Chibineko Kitchen.

A meal for three.

'Please eat.' At Kai's encouragement, Kumagai and Sumire took up their chopsticks again.

'Itadakimasu.'

Kumagai put his palms together once more. The bowl in front of him was hot to the touch, and steam wafted upwards. His appetite, which had left him just moments before, returned.

Back when he had lived with Sumire and Shoma, the long hours Kumagai had worked had meant he could eat and eat and still be hungry. He would make this post-hotpot curry partly to cure his son's dislike of vegetables, and partly to satisfy his own appetite. It was like a second course. And if they didn't finish it all, they would put the rest in the fridge for Shoma to eat the next day. 'I love yesterday's curry, it's super good!' he would say.

Kumagai's heart ached, remembering those days. Scooping up the curry and rice in his chopsticks, he carried it to his mouth, taking care not to drop any. 'Mmm . . .'

He could taste the fragrant spices, but the sauce was mild, as Kai had said. It coated the tender vegetables, their sweet flavours accented by the soy sauce. It was exactly like the shime curry he remembered.

He glanced up, about to remark on this to Kai, and then froze in shock.

*

Where the air had been perfectly clear a moment before, now the room was filled with a mist so thick Kumagai could no longer see out of the window.

'What . . .?' His question tailed off as he realised his voice sounded funny. Muffled.

Kumagai glanced around him, but he couldn't see Sumire or Kai. He hadn't heard them leave, but they had vanished.

'Is anyone there?' he asked, in the same muted tone.

'*Miaow*,' came the reply. It was Chibi. His mew was muffled too, but the little ginger-patched kitten was undeniably there, on the rocking chair.

He looked at Kumagai, gave another brief mew, and then jumped down from the chair and walked towards the restaurant door.

'Outside . . . right.'

Maybe Kumagai would find some explanation for these strange goings-on out there. He rose from his seat and overtook the kitten as he made for the door, thinking that he should take care not to let the little cat out; he'd feel terrible if Chibi escaped and went missing.

But when he looked down, he couldn't see the kitten at all. In the short time between moving from his seat to the door, the mist had grown so thick that now he couldn't even see his own feet.

This was seriously weird. *Perhaps the world is ending.* Kumagai was gripped by the feeling that something terrible was happening, and yet he opened the door as though being pulled irresistibly outside.

What he saw next made the breath catch in his throat.

'But that's impossible . . .'

There, outside the restaurant, was the hand-dug tunnel by Mishima Lake. Was he dreaming? Was he losing his mind? The sea had vanished. It could have just been hidden by the haze, but Kumagai could no longer hear the waves, nor smell the salt breeze. All he could see before him was a road leading to the mouth of the tunnel, and the surrounding rock and trees.

As he stood there, completely dazed, he heard the faint sound of a cat mewing. He knew at once that it wasn't Chibi. These mews sounded different, and they were coming not from the restaurant, but from inside the tunnel.

Kumagai had a good ear, perhaps from his years as an actor, and he recognised the sound. 'Kotaro?' he called, and was met with another answering mew.

A calico cat – black, white and ginger – trotted out from the tunnel. Yes, it *was* the cat Kumagai had so often seen in the park near their old Tokyo flat, the one that Shoma had named Kotaro.

'What are you doing here?' Kumagai asked.

The calico cat looked back over its shoulder and gave a '*Miaow*', as though it was calling to someone. And then Kumagai heard footsteps.

They were light and quick, like a child's.

Kumagai's heart began to race. 'It can't be . . .'

And as though summoned by the words that had escaped Kumagai's lips, a boy emerged from the tunnel.

'Hi, Dad.'

Somehow Kumagai knew what had to happen next: he was going to explore the hand-dug tunnel by Mishima Lake with his son.

'Come on, Dad, let's go!' Shoma said eagerly.

And Kumagai wanted to. But there was something weighing on his mind. 'Shoma, is Mum with you too?' he said. He couldn't see Sumire anywhere.

'No. We're going on a manly adventure. She wouldn't get it,' Shoma replied.

It was the same thing he had said in life – but Kumagai knew that Sumire would want to see their son. 'Shoma, come on now,' Kumagai tried to persuade him, but Shoma wasn't listening.

'Mum's fine. See you inside, then!' the boy said, and set off down the tunnel.

'Hey, don't—!' Kumagai called, but there was no reply. He realised that the calico cat had disappeared, too. Other faces arose suddenly in his mind: Yuito, Nanami. They were all gone. If he wasted any more time, he might lose sight of Shoma too. People vanished all too easily.

'Wait!' he called, and started towards the tunnel in pursuit of his son.

The road to the tunnel stretched out from the door of the Chibineko Kitchen. There were weeds growing at the wayside, and fallen leaves littered the ground. At the tunnel entrance, a warning sign read: DEAD END. NO THROUGH ROAD.

It looked like an ordinary, disused road tunnel. It was only knowing that it had, in fact, been dug by hand long ago that made people venture in.

Kumagai stepped inside. The other end wasn't visible through the gloom, but the tunnel did seem to lead somewhere, because he could feel a faint breeze. It smelled not of the sea but of the forest.

Surely this can't be just a dream or a hallucination.

Moving forward at a jog, Kumagai caught sight of Shoma ahead of him. His son was walking along with a spring in his step, craning his neck to look up at the rough-hewn, rocky walls and ceiling.

'Watch your step. You'll fall and hurt yourself,' Kumagai called to him.

'I won't hurt myself, Dad! I'm already dead,' Shoma replied with a laugh.

Kumagai felt tears sting his eyes, but he set his mouth firmly and held them back. A father mustn't cry in front of his son. 'Course . . .' he replied, forcing the word out.

'Hurry up, Dad!' Shoma called.

'All right, I'm coming.'

Kumagai quickened his pace until he was running through the dark tunnel. He heard Shoma's voice up ahead, teasing him.

'Dad, watch your step. You'll fall and hurt yourself.'

It felt to Kumagai as though the darkness would go on for ever, but then he reached a bend in the tunnel. Beyond the bend there were lights fixed up on the wall, and their warm glow went a little way to repelling the gloom. Kumagai pressed on until he caught up with Shoma.

'You're out of breath! You need to get more exercise, Dad.'

'You're right,' Kumagai panted, walking now alongside his child. He was so small, Shoma – his head didn't even come up to his father's chest.

Both Kumagai and Sumire were tall, and Kumagai had thought Shoma would overtake him one day – that one day he'd be the one looking up at his son. But that day would never come. Time had stopped for Shoma; he would be a child for eternity.

And then suddenly Shoma was speaking: 'I'm sorry, Dad.'

'Sorry? What for?' said Kumagai.

'Sorry for dying before you.' All his bounce of a few moments ago was gone; it was as if Shoma was shrinking into himself, his little body smaller than ever.

'Shoma . . . it wasn't your fault.' It was all Kumagai could do to get the words out.

The thought that his son had been blaming himself all this time was too much to bear, and his vision blurred with tears. Squeezing his eyes shut and trying to force his sobs back, he was engulfed in darkness once again, a black so deep it surely couldn't be just the shadow behind his eyelids.

And then Kumagai experienced one more miracle.

*

It was like a dream within a dream. As Kumagai stood, with eyes still closed to stop his tears spilling out, he heard a woman speak.

'Shoma is such a kind boy.'

It was indistinct, but he could tell who it was at once. It was Sumire, her voice tender as she spoke the name of their child.

Kumagai kept his eyes shut and listened, afraid that if he opened them her voice would fade away.

'He's just like you, you know. You could have left me and gone on your knees to the agency boss. He would have taken you back and made you famous.' Her voice came to him through the darkness.

She had said the same thing back when she was pregnant.

'You should have forgotten all about me,' she told him.

Sumire had cried for Kumagai when he had quit acting, thinking only of him, though she had been forced to retire from the industry in the same way. She had even apologised to him.

After a silence that lasted several seconds, Sumire's voice came out of the darkness again. 'You must regret marrying me.'

'*Never.*' The word came out before Kumagai could think, and he truly meant it. His theatre work made up for the career in television he had sacrificed. And if he hadn't married Sumire, they would never have had that life together. Shoma would never have been born.

Being Sumire's husband, being Shoma's father, had brought him so much happiness, it was as though he had been born into this world just to meet them. Kumagai still felt that way after everything that had happened, and he knew he always would, right through old age and until the end of his days.

'Do *you* regret it?' Putting the question to Sumire, Kumagai suddenly realised he had always wanted to know. After all, if they had never met she probably would have continued acting. She might have been quiet and unassuming, but she had real talent too; she would likely have been an outstanding supporting actress, the kind who found herself with more and more work as she got older. 'You must regret it, surely,' he said once more, but she gave the same reply he had.

'Never.' Her tone was earnest, unequivocal. 'Life with you and Shoma was wonderful.'

She sounded wistful, but there was something too clean-cut about her words, as though she were drawing a line under that time.

As though she were saying goodbye.

'Hey—' Anxiously, Kumagai called out, but there was no reply. He called to Sumire again and again, but there was only silence. Like the quiet after a television has been switched off.

When he opened his eyes, he saw Shoma's face.

'Dad, come on, we've got to go.'

'Right.' Kumagai nodded. He said nothing of Sumire, just set off again along the tunnel with his son.

When they reached the end of that section of the tunnel and emerged into the light, they could see Mishima Lake stretching out to their right. The second section of the tunnel, which was straight – they could see sunlight streaming in at the far end – began again close by. It was supposed to open out onto an expanse of autumn colours; a sight so beautiful it would hardly seem real.

'We *have* to see it,' Shoma had said eagerly, before the accident. But now he stopped at the mouth of the second tunnel, and made no move to go in.

'We can't go any further,' he said to his father.

'Oh?'

'The remembrance meal will be cold soon.'

It was immediately clear to Kumagai what Shoma meant, though he wished it wasn't. His son was telling him that he had to return to the world beyond.

Kumagai had always known that the miracle couldn't last for ever, that the dead can't stay in the world of the living. He had heard it from Nanami, and from Kotoko. Though he hated to part with Shoma, he would have to accept it. But first there was something he needed to say.

'Are you going to leave without seeing your mum?'

Kumagai wanted Sumire to have the chance to see Shoma. Her grief, he knew, was as deep as his own. He was on the verge of saying firmly, *Go and see her*, when Shoma replied.

'Mum will be all right.'

'What do you mean, she'll be all right?'

'I've already seen her.'

Kumagai closed his mouth. Then, 'I see . . .' And he did. He hadn't just imagined Sumire's voice back inside the tunnel. She had been there too, in that dark, magical place.

'I made sure I spoke to her. So it's okay. Don't worry about Mum,' Shoma reassured him, before changing topic. 'Dad, I have a favour to ask you.'

'Go ahead. Whatever it is, ask,' said Kumagai.

The only possible response – what parent would refuse to hear the wishes of their dead child?

208

'Well, I left this world, your world, so soon I don't know much about it. So I'll want to hear all about your life. What it's like turning into a doddery old man, stuff like that.'

'Doddery?'

'Yeah. I think we'll see each other again. I mean, it'll be way, way in the future – but when we do, I'll have loads of things I want to ask you.'

At this, the tears that had been gathering in Kumagai's eyes spilled over. He couldn't help it; his son was telling him to go and live a long, long life.

'I think it's super cool, getting to live until you're all old and creaky.'

'I . . . I don't know if I'll make it that far,' Kumagai replied, half sobbing.

'It's all right. You will. You're the greatest dad in the world,' Shoma declared. He sounded so full of strength and vitality, his voice brimming with confidence.

But their time was nearly up. Shoma was growing faint, like smoke dissipating into the air. Before Kumagai could say anything, he continued: 'For me, it was all over in a flash. But that's okay, because it was so much fun.'

'I . . . I had . . .' *I had fun too*, Kumagai wanted to say, but his voice wouldn't come. His chest hurt so badly he thought it would split open.

But still he smiled. Because it's a parent's job to smile for their child, no matter the struggle, no matter the pain.

'Bye bye, Dad.'

'See you, Shoma,' Kumagai managed to say. He balled his hands into fists, his nails biting into his palms, and held back the sobs rising in his throat.

'Yeah. See you,' Shoma said.

Kumagai had lost sight of his son now. He could only hear Shoma's light footsteps, fading into the distance. And then he was alone.

Unclenching his fists, Kumagai covered his face, hot tears trickling through the gaps between his fingers.

How long had he stood there crying at the mouth of that second tunnel?

The next thing Kumagai knew, he was sitting in his seat by the window of the Chibineko Kitchen. Outside, sea and sky were expansive and blue, and the black-tailed gulls ambled along the sand. Both the rocky tunnel and the mist had vanished.

'Some tea for you.' Kai's voice was clear as day.

Kumagai turned to the seat next to him and there sat Sumire. The bowls of curry and rice were still there on the table, now completely cold; the remembrance meal laid out at the place opposite was untouched.

But not everything was exactly as it had been. Sumire's eyes were red: traces of the miracle. Kumagai didn't need to ask her what had happened. She had just parted from her child for a second time – of course she had wept. His own face must be swollen from crying too.

'Here you are.' Kai set the teacups down. Green tea for Kumagai, roasted barley tea for Sumire.

Kumagai took a sip, moistening his throat, and then he turned to his estranged wife.

'I saw Shoma,' he said.

'So did I . . .' Sumire said with a nod, before falling silent.

Kumagai didn't feel like talking either. The restaurant was hushed. He looked at the old clock and saw that the morning was almost over. The Chibineko Kitchen only stayed open for breakfast.

Well, time to head off, he was about to say, when Sumire opened her mouth as though to make a confession.

'I'm getting married.'

Kumagai sat for a moment digesting her words. Then, 'I see,' he said, quietly. He wasn't surprised. Shoma's words still echoed in his ears. *Mum will be all right.*

The boy had known his mother was getting married again. And Kumagai could guess why she was drinking barley tea.

'You've noticed,' Sumire said. One hand rested on her stomach. Kumagai remembered her doing the same thing when she had been carrying Shoma.

Though this new child would not be Kumagai's, it would be a little brother or sister to Shoma. Maybe that was why Sumire had wanted to come here, to tell their son the news. Kumagai could guess how Shoma had reacted. He must have been delighted. After all, what had Kumagai heard Sumire say inside the tunnel? *Shoma is such a kind boy.*

Kumagai's eyes grew hot again. He'd done nothing but cry since he'd arrived at this restaurant. Shoma would have laughed to see him carry on like this.

'I wasn't able to make you happy. But I hope from now on, you will be,' Kumagai said, wanting to end with a remark worthy of the man who had once been her husband.

'That's not your business,' his ex-wife replied bluntly. But her voice wasn't barbed. 'I *was* happy when we lived together, you know.'

'I see,' Kumagai said again. He had been happy too. But he didn't say it, out of respect for the man who would be Sumire's new husband. Or perhaps it was jealousy that stopped him. His foolish, manly pride.

And then he heard Shoma's voice again. *No, Dad. It's a manly adventure.*

But Shoma was gone. *I must be hearing things*, Kumagai thought, a wry smile on his lips.

Sumire glanced at the old clock and then stood up. 'I'd better be off.'

She had someone waiting for her. She was building a new family. Only now did Kumagai's chest begin to ache at the thought. He loved Sumire with all his heart, but he would probably never see her again.

'Take care.'

'You too.'

Sumire left the Chibineko Kitchen, and Kumagai watched her from the window as she walked away down the seashell path. 'Take care,' he said once more, as her figure grew smaller and smaller. Even though he knew his voice wouldn't reach her.

She didn't look back.

Kumagai was alone now, but he didn't feel as though he had been left behind. He had made Shoma a promise. He would live life to the full, and then he would tell his son all about it when they met again in the next world.

Shoma had died without ever seeing his father on stage. Kumagai had never told him about the TV drama, either.

You're the greatest dad in the world, Shoma had said, and Kumagai wanted to prove him right. He wanted to be able to speak of what he'd achieved with pride. There was more to acting than just being on TV, anyway. He would start by writing a script, he decided. And with that script, he would make his comeback on the stage. True acting talent shines through even when you're old and doddery. He would begin in minor roles; he might be the head of the theatre company, but he would prove that he could win the lead parts on his own merits.

He was wasting time – now that he had made his decision, even these moments spent sitting sipping tea seemed too precious to spare.

'I'll stop by again. I'll come for a normal meal,' Kumagai said to Kai as he got up. And he meant it; the Chibineko Kitchen was as lovely as ever, even if it did have a new owner. He wanted to visit Nanami's grave, too.

'Thank you very much for your visit. We look forward to seeing you again.'

'Well—' Just as Kumagai reached the door of the restaurant, Chibi gave a short '*Miaow.*'

214

The cat sounded as though it was trying to tell him something, but Kumagai had no idea what.

Kai, however, seemed to understand. 'Kotoko will be here shortly. I wonder if you would like to see her before you go?'

Kumagai had completely forgotten about Kotoko, even though she was the one who had booked his remembrance meal. After a moment he said, 'I won't hang around for her just now. I see her most days at rehearsal anyway.' Kotoko might have looked like a daydreamer, but she was surprisingly astute. She wouldn't fail to notice that he had been crying. The thought was an embarrassing one.

'I understand,' Kai said, composed as ever.

Kumagai was struck by the thought that he could hardly believe Kai was younger than himself. He felt a sudden urge to tease him, to ruffle the man's calm.

'It hurts, you know. Parting from the woman you love,' he said.

Kumagai was fairly certain that Kotoko had feelings for Kai; he could tell by the way she looked when she talked about him. Kumagai had always known how to read people's faces. He wasn't sure whether Kai recip-rocated Kotoko's feelings, but he hoped to prod the young man into revealing himself in his answer.

Kai could have laughed and brushed off the remark, but he didn't. He paused for a moment at Kumagai's unexpected words, and then recovered his steady, serious expression.

'I will take care to avoid that happening,' he said, looking Kumagai in the eye.

And with that, Kumagai understood: their love was mutual. He was sure the two would find happiness. He'd let them get there at their own pace.

'Sorry – that one wasn't my business either,' he said.

This was no time to be sticking his nose into other people's affairs of the heart. He waved at Kai as he left the Chibineko Kitchen behind. The kitten mewed a goodbye, but Kumagai didn't look back.

Kumagai walked away along the empty sands. He could hear the waves, the calling of the gulls. The bright December sunshine streamed down. As he squinted in the light, he saw Kotoko walking towards him. *So much for leaving without speaking to her.*

Her clothes and appearance were simple, as always, with that slightly retro elegance. When she spotted Kumagai, she called out to him. 'Are you on your way home?'

'Yeah, just heading back. Got a script to write,' he replied. In fact, he thought, he might be able to cast Kotoko in a lead role in one of his plays. Not anytime soon, of course: she didn't have the experience yet, and keeping an audience rapt requires a lot of skill. But people grow, and Kumagai was expecting great things of her. He was sure there would come a time when her ability surpassed her brother Yuito's.

But he didn't say any of this to Kotoko. He was planning to make his comeback as an actor, so maybe there would even be some friendly competition between them. Who knew what the future would hold? Whatever happened, he would have a story to tell Shoma.

Nothing had changed, all he had done was to turn his gaze forward; yet now the landscape ahead of him looked different from before.

'Funny old thing, isn't it? Life.'

'Um . . . is it?' Kotoko replied curiously, but Kumagai didn't intend to explain all that had happened to him.

'Yes. You should ask Kai about it.'

'All right,' Kotoko replied, though a question remained on her face.

Kumagai's remark had come out of the blue, he realised, but he meant what he said: everyone should have someone they could talk about life with.

'Well, see you,' he said, and set off again along the sand.

'Nice work today,' Kotoko called after him. It was what the theatre group always said to each other.

Kumagai didn't turn around, but he raised a hand as he continued along the deserted beach. He heard Kotoko's footsteps resume behind him, moving off in the direction of the Chibineko Kitchen and then fading out of earshot.

The seaside town was as quiet as ever. Kumagai's footsteps crunched loudly on the sand. Tears filled his eyes, blurring his view. But he didn't stop; he just kept on walking forwards.

A special recipe from the Chibineko Kitchen

Shime no Kare: Curry using leftover hotpot

Ingredients (serves 4)
- Leftover hotpot (such as yosenabe, mizutaki or sukiyaki)
- Shop-bought Japanese curry stock – to taste
- Soy sauce – to taste
- 4 servings of rice

Method
1. Simmer the leftover hotpot until the vegetables are tender.
2. Turn off the heat and break the curry stock into the hotpot.
3. Turn the heat back on and continue to cook, stirring continuously, until the curry stock is thoroughly mixed into the hotpot.

4. Season to taste with soy sauce.

5. Dish the rice into bowls and ladle the curry over the top.

Tips

As you will be seasoning with soy sauce, you may want to use just a modest amount of curry stock to avoid the dish becoming too salty.